DADDY'S UNEXPECTED GIFT

AVA GRAY

ALSO BY AVA GRAY

C ONTEMPORARY ROMANCE

Mafia Kingpins Series

His to Own

Harem Hearts Series

3 SEAL Daddies for Christmas

Small Town Sparks

Her Protector Daddies

The Billionaire Mafia Series

Knocked Up by the Mafia

Stolen by the Mafia

Claimed by the Mafia

Arranged by the Mafia

Charmed by the Mafia

Alpha Billionaire Series

Secret Baby with Brother's Best Friend

Just Pretending

Loving The One I Should Hate

Billionaire and the Barista

Coming Home

Doctor Daddy

Baby Surprise

A Fake Fiancée for Christmas

Hot Mess

Love to Hate You - The Beckett Billionaires

Just Another Chance - The Beckett Billionaires

Valentine's Day Proposal

The Wrong Choice - Difficult Choices

The Right Choice - Difficult Choices

SEALed by a Kiss

The Boss's Unexpected Surprise

Twins for the Playboy

When We Meet Again

The Rules We Break

Secret Baby with my Boss's Brother

Frosty Beginnings

Silver Fox Billionaire

Taken by the Major

Playing with Trouble Series:

Chasing What's Mine

Claiming What's Mine

Protecting What's Mine

Saving What's Mine

The Beckett Billionaires Series:

Love to Hate You

Just Another Chance

Standalone's:

Ruthless Love

The Best Friend Affair

PARANORMAL ROMANCE

Maple Lake Shifters Series:

Omega Vanished

Omega Exiled

Omega Coveted

Omega Bonded

Everton Falls Mated Love Series:

The Alpha's Mate

The Wolf's Wild Mate

Saving His Mate

Fighting For His Mate

Dragons of Las Vegas Series:

Thin Ice

Silver Lining

A Spark in the Dark

Fire & Ice

Dragons of Las Vegas Boxed Set (The Complete Series)

Standalone's:

Fiery Kiss

Wild Fate

BLURB

When a billionaire becomes a child's legal guardian overnight, I'm plugged into the messy situation.

Only to make it messier.

Sterling Alexander was supposed to be a project.

You know, a new parent who didn't know anything about parenting?

As a social worker in family services, I wasn't permitted to stare at his gorgeous abs like I wanted to sleep with him.

And yet, I stared.

Oh, I also slept with him… *multiple times.*

The one thing I had promised myself not to do was fall in love.

Surely, that could remain off-limits, right?

Wrong.

The guy had a billion dollars along with my heart.

And now he was about to receive another gift…

A gift that would make him a parent yet again.

1

STERLING

S weat stung my eyes. That was good. That was the goal.

I dodged and jabbed, blowing spit and sweat out with each puff of breath. Heavy metal music screamed, and the beat pounded out the driving rhythm of my workout. Left, right, feign right again, uppercut.

My fist smacked into the leather bag. It swayed before snapping back into position, held in place by heavy-duty bungee cords.

I kept the lights low and the thermostat cranked. This workout needed to be brutal, needed to push my limits. I wasn't working out for fun. This was therapy, and it did so much more for my mental wellbeing than sitting around in a well-furnished office pretending to talk pleasantries.

I wasn't the type to vocalize the darkness inside. That led to emotions, and emotions were not welcome. Anger was welcome, but not in polite society. I was nothing if not polite when dealing with other people. But on my own…

I pushed my body through the paces. This was my anger management, this was where I let out my rage. My sins were absolved in a baptism of sweat. I was awash in sweat.

I punished the large upright bag, feeling each impact on my knuckles. Inside the light boxing gloves, my knuckles were wrapped, but after this afternoon, they would be red, if not swollen. That wouldn't do. I'd have to ice my hands. A gentleman didn't have the meaty hands of a pugilist.

Gentlemen were boring. I should know. I was raised to be one. Raised to be charming, mild-mannered, to not raise my voice, to never…

I growled and attacked my opponent with a series of fast-pounding, quick jabs. The stupid bag stayed in place and took the beating of my frustration and petty annoyances of the past week that needed exorcising. There were also ghosts that needed to find their way out of my mind and thoughts.

Outside these walls, I was the man my parents raised me to be. Responsible, smart, quick-witted, but never sarcastic. I excelled at the pleasantries of small talk, knew appropriate social dances, which fork was for salad, and to always stand when a lady entered the room. I also knew the difference between a woman and a lady. It was a fine line of social nuance, but it also meant I knew when to treat a woman like a lady and when to treat her as an equal.

As I brutalized the punching bag, I was free from the social constraints that were forced upon me.

When the current song ended, I shifted from the punching bag, grabbing a jump rope. I shifted from anaerobic to aerobic, keeping the burn going, the sweat flowing. Once I found the rhythm, I was able to level up so that I practically ran in place as the rope swirled around me. I only stopped when one of the handles slipped from my hand.

Taking that as a clear sign that it was time to switch activities, I dried my hands on the towel hanging at my waist. Lifting my arms, I began working with the smaller speed bag that hung at eye level.

The lights in the home gym flickered on. Ignoring the simple request for my attention by my assistant, Wayne, I continued with the rapid rotational punches with the speed bag. The anaerobic burn seeped deep into my shoulder muscles, not that I had any fat to burn off.

The lights flickered off then on, like the silent announcement in a theater. Time to stop whatever is going on and attend the show. Wayne knew I did not like being interrupted.

I dodged right and smashed a left hook into the speed bag before I turned to glare at him.

"This had better be good," I said as I plucked the earbud from my right ear.

"You have a delivery," he said in his precise, clipped tones.

"So, sign for it." I pushed the earbud back in.

"I'm afraid I can't, Mr. Sterling." His voice was muffled behind the wall of music the earbuds created.

"What?" I pulled both out this time. "Is it a subpoena?" I couldn't think of any reason I should be served with a court order.

"No, it is not. But it is something I cannot accept on your behalf."

"Fine." I pulled the towel from my waistband and wiped the sweat running down my face. Extending my arm, I gestured for him to lead the way.

I jogged up the stairs and passed him on the way to the front. "Do you have tip money? I don't have any cash on me. They probably want a tip. Why didn't the concierge at the front handle this?"

"I don't believe they are expecting a tip. I'm afraid it has to do with your sister."

9

I paused and let out a heavy breath. Argene. I nodded. She was one of the reasons behind today's brutal workout. She probably would be in my mind during future weekly sessions for a while.

"She's already dead," I said without emotion. "What other problems can she cause?"

Wayne didn't answer. He raised his brows and lifted his hand, indicating that I would find out soon enough. I tightened my abs, expecting that this could be the final delivery, her ashes. The autopsy had been completed weeks ago. The level of alcohol and other substances in her system had been off the charts. The cocktail indicated she was only trying to have a good time, not kill herself.

That tracked. Argene loved to party, much to the detriment of her ability to make smart choices. I had been cleaning up after her for years, dragging her to rehab centers, only to have her run away. I took care of Argene because she managed to do what I had not. She freed herself from the expectations that came with our family name.

Once she turned twenty-one, I washed my hands of her. She broke my heart one too many times, and I now had a business and reputation to protect. She was going to do what she wanted. It was clear that I would never be able to change that. So, I distanced myself, physically and emotionally.

Our parents were long dead. She had missed Dad's funeral. Apparently, she had been out partying in international waters and missed the helicopter that would have gotten her back to an airport.

Unable to completely cut Argene off, I managed her trust so that she would always have funds, no matter what she got herself into, but I stopped caring whether she went on a bender on a yacht in the Mediterranean or sequestered herself in an Ashram looking for enlightenment. I no longer traveled all over the world dragging her drunken, limp body back to the States to get her sober.

It's not what she wanted. She had been old enough to make her choices, as bad and embarrassing as they might have been. I was pretty sure this was not what she had wanted either, to be a pile of ashes kept in a little box.

The little box was the worst of it. I would make arrangements to scatter her ashes somewhere. The real question was where? Argene had struggled to be a free spirit, but she was trapped by a family and expectations she didn't know how to live up to.

I'd take her ashes next time I could get a long weekend away. She had always loved Ibiza. Maybe it was the beaches, maybe it was the parties. The last summer before she discovered drugs, we had spent on the Balearic Islands. That had been the last summer Mom had been alive. The last time I think Argene had been truly happy.

"You need me to sign for a package?"

The stern looking woman at the door held a pudgy baby against her hip and a clipboard out to me. "You're Sterling Alexander?"

"That's me." I took the clipboard and scribbled my name next to the arrow indicating an empty line. "Is it take your kid to work day?" I asked, looking at the kid. It was cute, if you like that sort of thing, with big eyes and little lips all puckered up.

I looked around and did not see a box or a bag on the floor. "You have a delivery for me? Is it Argene?"

"No." She shifted and placed the kid in my arms.

I took the kid, expecting the woman needed to get access to my delivery.

"Her mother was Argene Alexander. You're her closest relative."

"What?" I looked at the child in my arms. "What am I supposed to do with a baby?"

"I suggest you feed her and change her diaper."

2

CECELIA

"**D**r. Gareth highly recommended you, Cecelia."

My gut clenched as I followed my new supervisor down the hallway. I was glad Dr. Gareth gave me a good recommendation, but the fact that Greta Nelson seemed to know who he was, and the tone in her voice indicated the recommendation came with a certain level of expectations, made me super nervous.

This was my first job outside of the writing lab at school. Being a writing tutor had barely been a job. I mostly showed other students how to run their papers through a plagiarism checker and how to use the campus version of Pro Writer Aid. I hadn't even held a job at a fast-food place.

"You know Dr. G?" I asked.

"We like to hire State graduates. We know they've received a proper social services education. Dr. Gareth served as our board president a few years ago. When he's willing to recommend a recent graduate, we pay attention."

I guess understanding Dr. G's eccentric sense of humor had paid off. My aunt had always preferred dry British humor television or obscure science fiction movies. So, that's what I grew up watching. I got his references when everyone else in class would sit and stare at him and wonder how *Lost in Space* commentary was considered philosophy. *Lost in Space*, not so much, but *Forbidden Planet* was definitely a reference.

Greta walked with rapid determination, a pile of file folders clutched to her chest. She pointed to various places in the office as we continued to walk.

"The ladies' room is down that way." She pointed in one direction, and then in another. "Copier and coffee are at the end of that hall."

We entered a large workspace with two rows of desks, not even cubicle walls separating them. She stopped next to the third desk in the second row. "You're here."

I glanced around the workspace. Most of the desks were under piles of papers. Only a few other workers were at their desks. I turned a worried gaze to Ms. Nelson.

"Where is everyone?" I had heard agencies like this one were always underfunded and understaffed, but—I did a quick count—there were twelve desks. Three other people were in the room, and at least two of the desks were clearly used for document storage.

"The rest are out with their clients. You'll spend most of your time working directly with your assignments."

"Oh. I thought I was going to be more of an office worker. I guess I didn't realize," I managed to say.

"Don't worry, you'll be fine. We're starting you off small, only one client."

"But clients?" I interrupted. "I haven't had any training, Ms. Nelson."

"Call me Greta, and no, we don't have any training. You'll learn as you go." She opened and closed a few drawers, pulling out a stapler, a tape dispenser, and other office supplies. She set them out on display.

"You aren't even going to sit me in front of video training? Protocols?"

Geta flipped through her collection of file folders. She handed over a dark blue folder.

I opened it. It had photocopies in pockets and another set of photocopies clipped in with those poke and fold tabs instead of a three-ringed binder.

"This is the information you want. Read through everything before you visit with your client. These are the forms you will need to have completed." She handed me another folder. "Make copies. These are your masters. You'll copy a fresh set each time. If you accidentally forget and fill this set out, don't worry, there's a complete set of all originals in the copier room."

"Isn't everything online? Can't I just download the forms as I need them?" I asked.

Greta let out a sigh and then a little laugh. "This must all look so terrifying and old-fashioned. But it's temporary, I promise. We've been scrambling a bit since we had to relocate in a hurry. Our previous offices flooded, and we've simply been trying to catch up. The server room was completely destroyed. And we found out the hard way, the only thing that was stored in the cloud was our IT person's head. We're rebuilding from copies employees had saved to their laptops."

"That sounds horrible," I commiserated.

"Worse than horrible. We lost a lot in the flood, but we have no idea how much we had lost prior to that due to the incompetence of the department. It's leaving us in the dark ages."

I nodded. "Oh, okay. That makes sense." It was hard to have a database of documents when the database short-circuited.

"On the upside, you'll learn how to do things the old-fashioned way, pen and paper and filing documents in triplicate. So, if the network ever goes down again, you'll already know what to do without skipping a beat."

"I was told I'd be getting a laptop?"

"Oh, no. Not while the system is down. Nothing to access online," she said.

"So, you don't need me to help with data entry?"

"We need you to help with…" She took a moment to flip through the files in her arms. She pulled out one of the thicker ones. "Georgie Alexander," she announced as she handed over the file.

I accepted the folder and started to flip through pages of notes. A photo of a baby was clipped to the inside front of the file.

"Baby Georgie," Greta said. "Her mother was found overdosed. It's so sad, it really is. Her uncle has temporary emergency custody while the biological father is being located."

I trailed my finger down the edge of the photo. Georgie. She was adorable with short, looping curls, the biggest blue eyes I had ever seen, and a little cupid's bow of a mouth. She looked more like a baby doll than a human baby.

"You'll check in on the family and offer them assistance as they adjust," Greta continued, describing the basics of my assignment.

"What kind of assistance?"

"Anything, everything. In cases like these where guardianship was outlined in a living directive—"

"A what?"

"Directive. It's not exactly a will, but like a will. Georgie's mother indicated that her older brother would look after the child if anything were to happen to her or the father. And due to certain legalities, the estate is now attempting to locate the father, and we have to make sure the child is properly cared for."

"But if she's not in the system…?" I started to ask.

"The child isn't officially in the state's system, so we can't place her with a foster family. Those families have already gone through rigorous assessments. Georgie is one of our private sector cases. We are actually a private agency. You were aware of that, of course."

"So, I just show up and make sure Georgie is okay?"

Greta nodded. "It's my understanding that she was left with an uncle who was not prepared for her. It's all in the notes. You have an appointment tomorrow, so you have time to read up."

Greta eased her arm full of files onto the desk, sorted through them, and pulled a few more out, setting them aside. "That should be everything you need. I'll leave you to it. The green folder has your travel expenses and mileage forms."

"Thank you." I was pretty sure I didn't mean it. After all, she had just shoved me into the deep end of the pool without asking whether I knew how to swim. In this particular case, I did not. I didn't know what needed to be done during a home inspection. Was I only doing an inspection?

I sat down and put the tote bag I held over my shoulder on the desk in front of me. I looked at the file folders. Nothing was labeled. Everything was a different color. Opening the desk drawers, I located a Sharpie marker and sticky notes. I didn't know what the policy was for writing on the folders, so I labeled the sticky notes and plastered those to the fronts of the appropriate folders.

I separated the files into two stacks, one to make copies of and the other to read. I didn't even know what to do with half of the forms. I cracked open the folder with *PROCEDURES* scribbled across the yellow sticky on its front. Hopefully, after reading through this, I would know a little more about what to do.

I tried to review protocol, but my mind kept returning to Georgie. If she had a clear transfer of custody, why were we even involved? I set aside the blue folder and picked up the one with Georgie's photo inside it.

Her file read like a romantic tragedy, poor little rich girl lost in a bureaucratic system. Just as Greta said, we were involved because there seemed to be a biological father involved with the custody. He needed to be located, and from what I read, it looked like they didn't have his identity, but someone did.

Poor little girl.

I flipped the page and read the name of her uncle who had custody. Sterling Alexander. I gulped. No, that couldn't be right, not *the* Sterling Alexander who leveraged his family's fortune into an even bigger fortune through online streaming technology?

It was him. So, not poor at all.

3

STERLING

"**W**hen is the nanny supposed to arrive?" I pressed my fingers to my temples. A headache pounded through my brain. The baby had spent the morning wailing. She woke up crying, and she didn't stop.

Between Wayne and me, we managed to get her changed and into clean clothes. That didn't stop the crying. He held her on his lap as I tried to spoon applesauce into her mouth, and that also did not stop her crying. Nothing soothed the child.

By the time she passed out, I think we were all exhausted.

"I don't believe she's a nanny," Wayne said as he held out a bottle of headache reliever pills and a glass of water.

I tossed back double the recommended amount and then drained the glass.

"Then why are they sending someone out? I thought she said they were sending someone from the agency to help out. Sounds like a nanny to me," I muttered.

"Would you care for—"

"A Bloody Mary," I instantly requested. "Extra Tabasco."

"Is alcohol wise this early?"

"Consider it brunch. Fry up some bacon and stick a couple of slices in the drink. I don't think I can face super greens this morning." I stopped and turned to watch him. The man was unflappable. How was it that he didn't need a stiff drink after the morning we'd endured?

I stood in the living room and stared down at the sleeping kid. I guess calling her a kid was being generous. She still had the round face of a baby and didn't seem to be able to even walk yet.

She sprawled out on the floor, her pudgy little arms above her head. She slept where she'd collapsed. I didn't want her to fall, so setting her on the floor seemed like the best idea. She just sat there and wailed until she fell over from exhaustion.

"Me too, kid." Part of me sympathized with her. Best to just give up and sleep and try again later.

The smell of frying bacon wafted in from the kitchen. I followed the smell just in time to watch Wayne put the final touches on my drink.

"Oh, you're here. You drink," he said, handing it to me. "Is it wise to leave Miss Georgie alone?"

"She's asleep, and we're only a few yards away. It's not as if we have left the apartment with her sleeping on the floor."

I took my drink and sauntered back into the living room. He had a point, and the floor seemed so undignified. But I didn't want to risk waking her if I tried to move her. And where would I put her? She spent the night in a laundry basket next to my bed.

I squatted down and peered into her little face. She looked exactly like Argene had when she was born. They could be twins, or clones. I hadn't known what to do with Argene at that point, either. And it certainly wasn't as if our mother would have encouraged me to interact with a baby girl.

It wasn't appropriate, as she would have phrased it. I had been four-teen and struggling, like all teenagers stuck between being an adult and still wanting to be a kid. Dad would have said something a little harsher. Something like, 'Real men don't take care of babies, that's women's work. You aren't a woman, are you?' They were very tradi-tional in their ways. Something my dear Argene had railed against. Unfortunately, that had included going against me as well.

This sleeping baby on the floor was all I had left of Argene. There was some kind of symbolism with Georgie asleep in her misery on the floor and me looking down on her, uncertain of how to proceed. That summed up my relationship with Argene pretty well, uncertain how to proceed.

The intercom buzzed. Normally, I would ignore it, but my gut was already clenching with nerves waiting for someone to come and figure out what I was supposed to do with this child.

"The concierge said the woman from the agency is here. She is coming up directly," Wayne announced.

I headed toward the elevator. It pinged open, and a teenager stood there looking amazed and confused all at once.

"Mr. Alexander?" she asked Wayne.

I snorted. I stood up, lifting my glass toward her. "That's me. Sterling. You want a drink?"

She looked at me, a sneer across her pretty face. Her gaze then shifted to Wayne, back to me, and finally, to the sleeping baby on the floor.

She rushed from the elevator, unceremoniously dumped the armful of file folders on the nearest side table, and rushed to the baby, landing on her knees before putting her face right in front of Georgie's.

"She's asleep?" The woman twisted and looked back at where Wayne and I stood.

"Yes. You could have simply asked."

She stood and brushed the front of her skirt. I pretended that I didn't notice, or that I hadn't been staring at her curvaceous ass when she was on the floor.

"Why is she on the floor and not in a crib?" she snapped.

I let out a sharp breath. "She's on the floor because she passed out from crying. We've had a difficult morning. I did not want to disturb her. There is no crib."

"And how much vodka is in your Bloody Mary?" There was no dodging the judgmental tone in her voice. Maybe she was older than I first thought.

Lifting one eyebrow, I twisted to look at Wayne.

"None, Miss."

"What?" we both asked at the same time.

"None. I made it with non-alcoholic vodka. I figured with this morning's visit, it would be prudent," Wayne said.

Part of me was pissed I hadn't noticed vodka missing from the drink, and part of me was astonished at how this man had my back in little ways.

"Show me," the agency lady snapped.

Wayne tipped his head and led the way to the kitchen. "Mr. Sterling keeps a well-stocked bar," Wayne started.

"Oh, I'm sure he does," she retorted.

"That included provisions for his acquaintances who choose not to imbibe. When he is in training, Mr. Sterling also refrains from alcoholic beverages, though he still enjoys cocktails."

Once in the kitchen, he showed off the bottle of zero proof spirits.

"I have extra bacon. Would you care for me to make you one?" Wayne offered.

She glanced from the drink I still carried to the bottle and then smiled at Wayne. "Since I don't smell any coffee, if it's not a terrible bother, yes, please."

She turned to me, and the smile that illuminated her face immediately dropped away. "My apologies for jumping to a conclusion without having all of the facts, Mr. Alexander."

"Please, call me Sterling." I extended my arm, indicating we should return to the living room. I took a seat and indicated that she should as well.

She gathered her file folders back into her arms and perched on the sofa. The woman needed a tote bag if she was planning on hauling a file cabinet's worth of documents around.

"So, exactly how are you going to be able to help me out?" I asked. She didn't exactly look like a nanny, and I couldn't figure out how all that paperwork would be beneficial.

Georgie picked that moment to start squirming, and then her siren wail of distress was back.

I set my drink down and lifted her up. I had never been allowed to hold or play with Argene until she was older and walking. Her daughter sort of hung from her armpits with my hands around her tiny rib cage.

"That's not how you hold a crying baby!" the agency lady said, launching from where she sat.

She pulled the kid from my hands and immediately had her arms wrapped around the baby and began cooing and bouncing.

"She's soaking wet. Where is the changing station?" she demanded.

I shook my head.

"Diapers? Do you have any?"

"Miss." Wayne appeared suddenly with the diaper bag in hand.

"Thank you. Where do you change her?" she asked.

I shrugged. "Wherever."

When she rolled her eyes at me, I changed my mind again. She couldn't be more than nineteen. Why had they sent over a kid?

"Wherever? Like you just change her diaper on the couch, the kitchen table, the floor?"

"Oh, no, not on the table, but that would be the right height. So far, I've just changed her on the bed."

"She has a bed?"

"My bed," I clarified.

"Where's your bathroom?" she asked.

"I'll show you. This way," Wayne interjected.

She turned to follow him.

I followed her.

"When was the last time you gave her a bottle, or did she have anything to eat?"

"She had some applesauce last night. And we tried to give her some this morning, but she refused to eat."

"No bottles?"

I shook my head. "No one said anything about bottles."

Wayne opened the bathroom door. She brushed past him, set the diaper bag on the counter, and then placed Georgie next to it. The baby hadn't stopped crying, but she was much quieter. The young woman never took her hand off the kid as she rummaged through the bag and pulled out what looked like a mini yoga mat, and then a diaper. With what looked like professional skills, she had Georgie on the mat and her diaper changed in no time.

She then proceeded to remove the clothes that I had struggled to dress the baby in. She held them out. "This is wet. Also, the fabric is super scratchy. Has she been fussy?"

"Fussy would have been pleasant," I admitted.

"Mr. Alexander, it doesn't appear to me that you know what you're doing. My first report isn't going to look very good."

"Report? Who are you going to report me to? How about we start with who you are?" I asked.

"I'm so sorry. I was caught off guard with what appeared to be a disaster, and then your drink... My bad. I'm Cecelia Harrison from Child Services. I'm your case manager."

4

CECELIA

What the hell was Sterling Alexander thinking?

He stood there watching me change baby Georgie's diaper like it was some kind of performance art or something. His smirking face and the way he held that mock-tail, non-alcoholic drink made me think he was taking all of this as a joke. I wasn't laughing.

"Oh, I know, I know," I cooed at the poor darling. She was shaking, she was so upset. Having just woken up, she was confused, she didn't know where she was, and another stranger was talking to her.

"You speak baby?" Sterling quipped.

I glared at him with my best laser eyes. "I speak scared and hungry, and she is both." I hitched the little girl in close, wrapping my arms around her protectively. She needed to know that somebody was going to take care of her. "How do I get back to the kitchen from here?"

I asked the older guy. I had never met a butler in real life before. I barely believed they weren't something made up for superhero movies. I already made up my mind about Sterling Alexander. He skated through life on his charm, good looks, and family money. None of those were going to sway me, and they certainly had no effect on the sniffling baby in my arms.

She didn't care about money. She cared about comfort and food and security.

"Shouldn't you dress her first?" Sterling asked, making useless gesturing motions with his hands.

"She's hungry. She'll get food all over herself. I see no reason she needs to be dressed, only to have to clean her up again." I stopped as we entered the kitchen from a different direction than we had earlier. That time, I had been concerned with Sterling's day drinking. This time, I was looking out for Georgie and— "Where's her highchair?"

"She doesn't have one," Sterling admitted.

"Why not?"

His eyes went wide as he looked at me. The expressions that danced across his face were almost comical. Wide eyes made way to a wrinkled brow, and then stoic blandness. He looked at me with a complete lack of emotion. He was better looking when he felt things.

"The past day and a half have been a bit overwhelming. I expected you yesterday, and I was under the impression that your agency was to provide support."

"Support, yes. Furniture, no." I turned to the butler, Wayne. "I understand you have applesauce? Could you put together a small bowl of that, please? Do you have any cereal, or oatmeal?"

"We have quick oats. Would you like for me to prepare some?" he asked.

"Yes, make them sweet, with maple syrup if you have some."

"Isn't giving the kid sweets bad?" Sterling asked.

He could stay out of this conversation as far as I was concerned. I glanced over his expensive clothes and got a very wicked idea.

"We need her to eat. She doesn't have the same tastes as an adult, and I don't know her history beyond the specifics of how she came into your life. Was she raised without sugar and only home-grown, home-made organic foods, or did her mom put Coca-Cola in her baby bottle? You said she wasn't interested in eating earlier. Either she was just too upset"—I stroked her soft hair. She wasn't crying any longer, but she clung to me like a monkey— "or she didn't like the food. Let's try something she's more likely willing to eat. I don't know about you, but plain oatmeal isn't very appealing."

"The applesauce, Miss." Wayne set a small bowl on the counter and then placed a spoon next to it.

I glanced around. There was a full-sized table with chairs on the other side of a bar-like counter. I gave Sterling a focused look, darted my eyes to the bowl, and then nodded. "Right, I'm going to need your help. Come on."

I turned and expected him to be smart enough to grab Georgie's food and follow me. He set the bowl next to the chair I sat down in, keeping Georgie on my lap the entire time.

"Are you hungry? Let's try some applesauce, okay?" I got her situated and thought she was going to hurt herself the way she grabbed at my hand and bit down on the spoon. Both men received more laser eye glares from me. "Not hungry? Did you even try?"

Georgie was starving. I couldn't get the applesauce from the bowl to her mouth fast enough. It didn't take much time before we almost finished the bowl.

"How is that oatmeal coming?" I asked.

"Almost done, I am returning it to a boil," Wayne started.

"No!" I practically shrieked. "She can't have hot food the way adults can. She doesn't know about blowing on the spoon to cool it down. If it's too hot to go into your mouth straight out of the pan, it is far too hot for her. A good rule is fully cooked, fully re-heated, but not served warmer than body temperature. At least while you are learning."

"Learning?" Sterling asked.

"Yes, learning, and from what I walked into this morning, you have a great deal to learn if you are going to properly care for Georgie."

"But you seem to have everything under control," he pointed out.

Little did he know I was faking it and falling back on my extensive babysitting experience. I at least knew to give a baby comfort and to not put her in picture day scratchy clothes and not expect her to fuss.

"Yes," I said, "but I'm the one taking care of her. You need to be able to do this without me around."

Wayne approached the table with a steaming bowl of oatmeal.

I looked flatly at him. "Really? It's steaming."

"Yes, Miss."

"Did you hear anything I just said? Take a clean spoon and put that in your mouth," I demanded.

Wayne retrieved a spoon, scooped up some oatmeal, and then began to blow excessively to cool down the bite. It wasn't until he put it in his mouth and made eye contact with me again that my previous words registered. "Oh, I see. I will pop this in the freezer for a bit. That should cool it down."

I rolled my eyes and shook my head. "Basic food safety rules apply, but you have to remember she is going to put her hands into food or shove it into her mouth without pause. It's your job as her adult to protect her, to care for her, to provide for her. If that's something you can't handle, we will make other arrangements for her."

Sterling's brow furrowed, and his expression darkened. "That won't be necessary. She will stay with me."

"Well, then, you had better start taking notes," I said.

Wayne brought the cooled oatmeal to the table.

I lifted Georgie and handed her to Sterling. At least he didn't hesitate to take her, but he didn't know how to hold her.

"Have you ever held a baby before?"

"No, I wasn't allowed to when my younger sister was born. It wasn't considered to be important. Men don't—"

"Ouch, really? Men don't? I… I'm going to shut up before I say something that will get me fired. Men do, all the time. And you're going to learn how to hold and feed her right now."

I directed him where to put his hands and how to support her so she felt secure. Georgie whimpered and reached out for me.

"You're fine," I told her. "Your uncle has you. He'll keep you safe." I lifted my eyes to Sterling's face. His eyes caught me off guard as he watched me intently. Momentarily flustered, I fumbled over my next few words and coached him through feeding her.

As expected, Georgie fought the oatmeal at first. Sticky globs of oatmeal went everywhere. I tried to suppress my smile as it got all over Sterling's designer slacks. Served the man right. But after a few tricky moments, the two of them figured out the whole feeding the baby and eating oatmeal routine.

"This will be easier next time when she's not hungry. You can try her with some rice and butter, and finger foods like Cheerios. She's old enough to be on solids. Cut things up small. She barely understands what her teeth are for, and she doesn't have any molars. How many sippy cups does she have?"

"There was one in the bag the lady from the agency gave us," Wayne answered since Sterling was focused on Georgie, as he should be.

I let out a sigh. "Do you have a pad of paper and a pen?" I asked. "We need to make some shopping lists, and the two of you have homework."

"Homework?" Sterling asked, looking up from feeding the baby.

"Yeah, you need some parenting books and to find out what she can and will eat. And don't just buy the books. Read them too. Now, let's start making a list of furniture and other items you'll need before I come back."

5

STERLING

After being put in my place by someone who was barely of the legal drinking age, I was left on my own with the baby again. This time, it was easier. The baby didn't cry so much. She was cute when she didn't sound like an entire fleet of fire truck sirens.

She sat on my lap, fed, clean, and recently woken from another nap. She seemed to sleep like a cat, at every opportunity. I scrolled through a list of parenting books, picking and choosing different titles. My online shopping cart was getting full.

I had no idea when I'd have the opportunity to read so much. "I can't believe that little girl gave me homework," I complained.

"She gave us both homework. I don't think she would appreciate being called a little girl, Mr. Sterling."

I hated being corrected by Wayne, especially when he was right.

Cecelia. Logically, I knew she had to be at least twenty-three or so. After all, her job did require a college degree. But she was diminutive and curvy. Almost to the point of being distracting. Good thing her harsh demeanor put the brakes on that train of thought.

"Shall I take Miss Georgie for a while?" Wayne asked.

I lifted the kid from my lap and handed her up. Wayne took her and immediately began babbling at her. He seemed more comfortable with her after Cecelia's visit as well. Maybe her brusque and forthright attitude had made us pay attention better.

"Miss Georgie should have some toys, a little dolly or something. There is nothing here to keep her occupied," Wayne said.

"I'll add it to the shopping list." It was a substantial list and growing. The many lists Cecelia had left with me had everything from food and dishes to clothes and furniture. "I'll probably only get about half the clothes. Georgie is only here temporarily."

I was thinking out loud. What was I going to do with all the baby furniture once the agency found her father?

Wayne was singing something and danced awkwardly around with the baby in his arms.

"You look like you're getting the hang of that," I commented.

"She is a sweet little thing. I feel bad for how yesterday and this morning went. I wasn't as helpful as I could have been," Wayne admitted.

Then again, I wasn't very good, either. "We were both ill prepared to deal with having a baby delivered. Didn't you ever work for a family with children?"

"Absolutely not, and I've never had any of my own. I am not well-versed in dealing with babies."

"You look like you're doing fine. However, I want to remind you that you are not a nanny." I joked a bit. "She is going to take all of your attention if you aren't careful."

"Maybe you should consider hiring a nanny?" Wayne suggested. He sniffed rather dramatically before shifting his attention back to the baby in his arms. "Please, hire a nanny." He stepped closer to where I sat scrolling through an online catalog of baby furniture.

I could smell the reason he was so emphatically in support of hiring a nanny.

"I'll buy you a new Lexus," I started.

"I already drive a Mercedes. A Lexus would be a downgrade," he responded with a wry chuckle.

"You can use the jet whenever you want," I countered.

He lifted a single judgmental eyebrow at my feeble attempt at bribery. It was not in his job description to change baby diapers.

"Fine." I pushed to my feet and took Georgie from him. My ward, my responsibility.

"While I'm changing her, take a look at that website. It looks like I can order a complete matching set of all the furniture we'll need. I'd like your opinion on the style and which room should be converted into a temporary nursery for Georgie."

I couldn't choose between the white set or the dark cherry. Neither fit my personal aesthetic. I didn't even know if I'd be able to find Mid-Century Modern baby furniture. Did such a thing exist? I needed furniture for Georgie immediately. That did not give me the luxury of contracting with an interior decorator to locate something I'd like in my penthouse.

Not feeling comfortable balancing Georgie on the bathroom counter as Cecelia had so aptly managed, I unrolled the changing mat on the bathroom floor. For such a small body, she created a rank mess. "How did all of this fit in your little body?"

Georgie made a gurgling sound, almost like a giggle. She started to kick her feet, but I grabbed her pudgy legs to stop her from flailing around.

I held my breath and got her cleaned up. I had to change her clothes, again. Maybe my decision to not order all of the clothes Cecelia had put on the shopping list wasn't the best plan. This was the baby's fourth outfit change today.

I tossed the soiled clothes into the tub and the diaper into the trash. "You're a little stink bug, aren't you?" I asked as I lifted her back into my arms.

She giggled and grabbed my nose. That was adorable.

"Let's get you dressed and go order you more clothes." I'm not sure why I was talking to her. It wasn't as if she could understand me or respond. She moved her mouth around as if she were talking, the occasional babbling sound coming out as her little tongue pushed in and out of her rosebud of a mouth.

Georgie's good nature seemed to last until we returned to the living room where my laptop was set up. The cranky version of the baby came back when I sat and started scrolling back through the websites to find the one where I had purchased clothing items from.

"Are you hungry again? You just ate, what? Four hours ago?" With a resigned sigh, I shifted her so I could carry her and picked up the laptop. The furniture and the clothes weren't going to order themselves.

"Did you manage to get a grocery delivery with baby food yet?" I asked Wayne as I changed my location from the living room to the kitchen table.

"I did. Not knowing what she would like, I got a variety. Is she hungry?"

I shrugged the best I could while still holding on to her. "I think so. Cecelia said Georgie should be able to feed herself some things," I said.

"Yes, but I believe that's something that maybe should wait until Miss Georgie has a highchair she can be secured into."

He had a point. "Fine, what have you got that I can feed her?"

"I'll have warmed up rice and chicken nuggets in about five minutes." Wayne continued to mutter under his breath, and I know I heard him complain about having chicken nuggets in his kitchen.

I didn't even know where to start. I pulled up another tab on my web browser and typed in *nanny services in Dallas*. The list that came back was extensive. Finding a nanny was going to be a challenge. I was going to have to reach out to Child Services to help me locate a nanny.

Nannies, clothes, food, furniture. This little girl required a lot of attention and money. How had Argene managed? She had plenty of money, but my sister had never been one to focus on long-term projects. Maybe that had changed once she had Georgie.

I watched the little girl on my lap as she grew fussy. I had loved my sister even though I didn't really know her. I never would now. Another missed opportunity.

Would I ever get to know the person this little girl would become? Would her father arrive and sweep her away, leaving me to wonder what she was really like? Would she grow up feeling like a caged bird like her mother had?

Wayne set a small plate in front of us. There was a pile of plain white rice and small cubes of...

"What is this?" I asked.

"Chicken nuggets and rice," he answered.

"I thought chicken nuggets were deep-fried blobs of formed meat."

"They are, Mr. Sterling. I cut these down to not be a choking hazard so Miss Georgie could feed herself."

As if she had been waiting for Wayne to let her know that was her food, Georgie lurched forward and grabbed at the food with both hands. Fortunately, I had a hand around her middle holding her on my lap. I was able to tighten my grip and prevent her from launching herself onto the floor.

Bits of food scattered. Her finer motor skills were not yet fully developed. But she did manage to get some of the food from her hands into her mouth. She reached for more of the cut-up chicken.

"She definitely likes chicken nuggets."

She also seemed to like the rice, though it made an even bigger mess.

"Wayne, I think we need to get a highchair in here immediately. I don't think Georgie can wait for one to be delivered."

"Yes, Mr. Sterling. I will take care of that."

6

CECELIA

"Greta?" I knocked on my supervisor's open door as I stepped into her office.

The space was small, lined with bookshelves along one wall and filing cabinets along the other two. Everything was piled high with stacks of files that needed to be put away, but as I understood it, all the space we currently had was used up.

"Come on in, Cecelia. How was your first day?" Greta didn't look up from the papers in front of her.

"Uh, that's what I wanted to talk to you about," I said. I picked up a smallish pile on the other office chair and set everything aside as neatly as I could before parking my butt in the chair. "My case is a bit of a mess."

"How so?"

"From all appearances, Mr. Alexander had no warning that he was going to be responsible for a baby. Isn't it customary to alert the guardian so they can prepare?"

"Mmm-hmm." Greta made a positive, please continue type of sound.

"When I got there, the child was asleep on the floor. And there was no, well, anything for her. I went through the notes, and... Did we really just hand over a child and say, 'Here, this is yours, take care of it until we find her father'?"

Greta looked up and me, her brow furrowed. "Let me see." She sorted through one of the stacks on her desk. When she found the folder she was looking for, she opened it and started flipping through the pages. "Ah, I see. Yes. Okay." She closed the folder and looked up, catching my gaze with her own.

"That's exactly what happened."

I gasped and prepared to have a rather indignant reaction. But Greta held my attention.

"It's stipulated in the will that Sterling Alexander take care of the child unless the father comes forward to do so. And the deceased's estate is being managed by lawyers making sure that's exactly what's happening."

"He had no baby furniture. No bottle, and only one sippy cup, and we just dumped a baby on him? I thought we were supposed to make sure that children were taken care of?" I had the hardest time believing that we were acting in the best interests of the child.

"Was the child being mishandled?" Greta questioned.

"She was asleep on the floor," I reminded her.

"Kids sleep on floors all the time. Was she injured?"

"She was distraught," I answered.

"Was she being neglected?"

I opened my mouth and shut it again. I couldn't tell her that when I got there the baby was asleep, and Sterling Alexander was standing there with a faux cocktail in his hands because his butler knew better than to serve him vodka while they were struggling to take care of a baby. I couldn't tell her because there was nothing wrong in that situation.

Neither man seemed to know what to do, but she had been in clothes, and they had appropriate foods available for her.

"They're totally clueless about taking care of a baby!" I blurted out.

Greta chuckled. "Most people are, especially when it's unexpected. How did you handle the situation?"

I cast my gaze around her office, suddenly feeling as if maybe I hadn't done enough. I tried to remember everything.

"I changed her, got her into some more comfortable clothes. I pointed out that babies and fashion don't mix. She needs to be in comfortable, soft fabrics. I showed both of them how to hold her, um..."

"Both? Was there someone else there?"

"Yes, Sterling Alexander has a butler. He called me Miss Cecelia. Very high-brow, posh. He was doing all of the cooking, so I made sure he understood what foods to start her on."

"That's good. She has two adults looking after her, someone who knows how to prepare food. So, exactly what is your concern?" Greta looked at me like I was the clueless one and not Sterling Alexander.

I blinked a few times, trying to realign my expectations with reality.

"I should follow up with him tomorrow," I said.

"Of course. We expect that of you."

"I guess I need clarification of how often I am supposed to be there? They are my only client. Shouldn't I have multiple clients?" I asked.

Greta nodded. "I see. Not in our group. You'll do some serious hand-holding until you decide your client is ready. Clearly, you don't find Mr. Alexander to be prepared for the task at hand. You're to be available to teach him how to care for the baby. You'll spend several hours a week based on his availability. Then, of course, you have all the reports you need to file. After that, we will have some other projects at the office for you to work on. But for now, we want you to focus on one family at a time."

I was confused. "I thought I'd have several cases to handle at a time," I admitted.

"Yes and no. I did mention the flood and losing our servers, right?"

I nodded. "Yes, you did."

Greta looked up at the ceiling. "How do I say this and maintain professionalism?" She let out a heavy sign. "As you can see, everything is a bit of a mess. When I say a bit, I mean the polar opposite. It's a cluster of intercourse."

I snorted with laughter. I couldn't help myself. "You mean a cluster fu—"

Greta waved her hands around wildly, stopping me mid-word. "We never say the F-bomb here. And yes, that is precisely what I mean. I can't assign you to other families at the moment because I can't access the records."

I felt my eyes go wide. What had I gotten myself into?

"It took us a week to get to where we are now. I expect that next week, we will be in better shape with the servers and having access to a functional database, except for the physical storage problem. That's going to take longer. In the meantime, you get to focus on one case at a time."

"Oh." It was all I could think of to say. This was not anything like what I thought I was getting into. I had images of overworked caseworkers visiting family after family, almost like a door-to-door salesperson. But I guess that was the difference between public social services and privately funded agencies. At least I had a job. "So, I'll actually be working with Sterling Alexander a bit more closely than I realized."

Greta nodded. "I'm going to warn you now, don't fall in love."

"What?" Sterling Alexander was a good-looking guy, but he was also an overinflated ego on legs. I was completely immune to whatever charms he thought he possessed. I didn't think there was any danger of falling in love with him.

"With the baby. It's always so hard not to bond with the kids in situations like these. You are so invested in their wellbeing, and sometimes, you end up spending a lot of time with the family. You aren't their friend. You're there to make sure they know and can do what it is they need. You're more like a life coach, but in a hands-on framework," Greta continued.

I nodded. "Georgie is adorable. I get what you're saying." I could see the danger of bonding with the baby. I already felt so much empathy toward her situation. And she was a little cutie with big eyes and the loopy curls I've only ever seen on babies. "I will harden my resolve against her and her manipulative ways."

"Babies aren't manipulative," Greta corrected me instantly.

"I know that," I stammered. "I was just saying, like, she would be the one trying to get me to bond with her on purpose. Sorry, bad joke, worst joke teller. There's a reason I'm not a comedian."

Greta gave me a half smile. I was wasting her time, and it was time for me to realize that and leave.

I stood. "Thank you for clarifying a few things for me. I'll go finish up the few reports I have and get them turned in."

"Remember, triplicate, and in the labeled baskets in the copier room," she said as waved me out of her office.

Triplicate? No, I'd be keeping a full set of those documents for myself. I needed to put together a filing system immediately at my desk. No one was in the room of desks when I returned. I sat and began sorting through what I needed.

There were a few office supplies not stored in the desk drawer that I wanted. I decided it was safe to rummage through the desks that were obviously just for stacking things on. I located a tape dispenser with tape and a staple remover.

I organized my folders in the drawer. I wasn't going to need to carry all of them back and forth, only a few of them. I needed to get a tote bag or something. And pads of paper. I needed pads of paper to take notes on.

I left my desk and went to the copier room to see if I could dredge up any more office supplies. I opened another cabinet that was crammed full of copier paper but no notepads. "What was this place like before their epic flood?" I really hoped it had been more organized than this and that everything would return to order soon.

7

STERLING

Cecelia from the agency sat on the floor and played peek-a-boo with Georgie. Her files were stacked up on the kitchen table, left from when she came to today's appointment as if she were braced for a fight. I didn't want to fight. I wanted to restore the peace and quiet I had prior to Georgie being foisted upon my life.

I very much was not set up to have a child. Something as simple as peek-a-boo had been beyond me. Of course, I knew how to play the game, cover my eyes and pretend I didn't know the baby was sitting in front of me, and then move my hands and act happy and surprised that I can now see the baby.

The problem was that it hadn't occurred to me. I had managed to hire a private investigator to find her father, but it hadn't occurred to me to play with her.

Interactions with Georgie had been pretty much left to eating, changing, and putting her to bed. She didn't seem interested when I attempted to read to her. She didn't understand most of anything I was saying, so what did it matter what I read to her? I was reading.

She wasn't interested in tech analytics or the financial reports I had to review. I had to read the material to keep up with the industry.

The baby books Cecelia had imposed on me told me to read to the baby.

I was doing my part. Georgie wasn't participating as expected.

And now she was climbing all over the woman from the agency, pulling her hands away from her eyes and giggling like this was the funniest thing she had ever seen. Peek-a-fucking-boo was hilarious.

"I was under the impression that you were going to inspect the living situation," I said sardonically. "I didn't realize this was a play date."

Georgie grabbed Cecelia's hands and pulled them away from her face. The baby let out a squeal of delight.

Cecelia did not shift her gaze over to me. She kept her smiling face on Georgie the entire time. Even the inflection in her voice was for the baby, though the words were definitely for me. "There is plenty of time for me to go through and assess the apartment—or is this a condo—for safety issues. Georgie was clearly in need of some interaction. Have you been reading to her?"

I grunted. "Yes, I read to her."

"Do you play with her?"

"I didn't realize that was a requirement," I admitted.

Cecelia's eyes flashed to meet mine. "She's a baby. Of course it's a requirement. She needs mental stimulation. Do you at least talk to her when you're feeding her?"

"What about? Market fluctuations in tech development? She's not exactly an expert." I crossed my arms and glared at the woman.

She made a pained expression, opening her mouth to berate me at first, but then she closed her mouth and sucked her lips in behind her teeth and closed her eyes. Was she counting to ten before speaking again? Had I pushed her to her limit?

If I had, her limits were very narrow. Why had someone like her gone into social services if she had no patience?

I watched and waited. Cecelia entertained me. Rude, I know, but her irritation with me was almost comical. I was tempted to poke at her just to see how she would respond. It was a juvenile response, a mechanism deep in the fiber of my being that had me acting out. Something inside drove me to pull on pigtails when I was a little boy and tease the girls with braces and training bras when I hit middle school. At some point, that need turned to something a bit more visceral.

I liked girls, and now I liked women. And there was something about Cecelia that brought out the little boy in me. It was as if I didn't know how to behave around her, so I wanted to annoy her. Tease her. Get her angry. Anything to have her give all of her attention to me.

"Miss Cecelia." I started speaking before she made it to number ten, or whatever she was counting to. "You are more than aware that I am out of my league here. Your agency knows this, but for some legal loophole my sister got her hooks into, I have custody of Georgie until her father can be located. Look around my place. I am not inclined toward children. My friends don't have kids. I am relying on your assistance to help me through this. So, no, it hadn't occurred to me to play with the baby."

Maybe if I threw myself on her mercy, she'd look at me again? I found the way light refracted in her eyes to be quite attractive.

She blew out a breath. I guess she was done counting.

"You can't be as hopeless as you're making yourself out to be. I've read almost everything in Georgie's file, and you would have been a teenager when her mother was born."

"I wasn't an integral part of Argene's childhood," I admitted. "My parents had strong opinions about what gender roles encompassed.

They thought my masculinity would be damaged if I played with a baby."

Cecelia blinked a few times. "Your father didn't play with you? He didn't change diapers?"

"Most definitely not." I chuckled.

Cecelia stood, brushed off her curvaceous backside, and then picked up the baby. "Okay, show me around. Let's see what you have managed to do. And I will try to think up a few crash course-style ways to get you up to speed with having a baby." She held Georgie out to me.

I stared at the baby and then shifted to look at Cecelia.

Cecelia let out an exasperated sigh. "Take her. You need to bond with her, not simply be her caretaker."

I took the baby. She fussed. We locked eyes. What was I supposed to do with this tiny human? She made the first move and grabbed and pulled on my nose.

"Ow." I grabbed her hands and pulled them from my face.

She cried.

"See," I complained. "She's always like this."

"Are you always like this?" Cecelia asked.

"What's that supposed to mean?"

"She was exploring your face. You don't look like anyone she knows."

"She grabbed my nose."

"Yeah. She grabbed mine too. It's kind of a thing babies sometimes do. If she hurts you, you need to be gentle."

I let go of Georgie's hands. She put them on my face again. This time, she ran them over the scruff of my beard before going for my nose.

"Why is it always the nose?" I grimaced.

"Gentle," Cecelia cooed. She eased the baby's grabby hands from my nose.

Georgie looked at Cecelia, and then back at me. Instead of grabbing my face, she petted me like I was a dog or a cat.

"Someone must have taught her that. To gently pat. She must have had a pet."

"I feel like a cat or something," I complained.

Georgie made a few noises. They were her attempts at talking. It took us a while, but she was able to almost say juice in a way that Wayne or I could recognize. These were different sounds than anything I had heard from her previously.

"Kitty?" Cecelia said.

Georgie repeated the sounds.

"She must have had a kitty cat."

"I'm not getting her a cat," I said.

"Best not. After all, you haven't gotten her any toys. Why don't you show me what you have managed to get her?" Cecelia said.

"You saw the highchair in the kitchen. Let me show you the bedroom."

"Did you manage to get a changing table?" Cecelia asked as she followed me down the hallway.

"I managed to get her an entire bedroom," I said. I opened the door to Georgie's room and stepped aside, allowing Cecelia to step in first.

Her entire face lit up as she looked around. "You managed to fully furnish a nursery in two days?"

"It's not my taste, but that doesn't really matter. I didn't have time to paint, and I felt that the white furniture went with the walls," I said.

Cecelia crossed the room and opened the dresser. "You even managed to get clothes."

"I have more on order. She goes through clothes much faster than I expected."

"Don't overbuy. Georgie will grow out of these sooner rather than later." She smiled, and this time, it was directed at me.

The same urge deep inside that had me wanting to poke at her now preened at the attention.

"You need more diapers," Cecelia said as she continued to inspect the room, opening drawers and dragging her fingertips over every surface, touching everything.

I suppressed the urge to growl and demand that she touch me the same way. I stepped in close behind her and inhaled her scent.

She turned suddenly. I hadn't realized I had gotten so close. There she was. Her chest brushed against mine as she took in a sudden, sharp breath. My gaze was drawn to her lips. Every time I tried to think of what my intentions were, I found myself looking at her lips and wondering what she tasted like.

I lowered my eyelids and leaned forward.

Georgie grabbed my nose again and her fingers pressed into my closed eyes. I flinched and stepped back. My initial reaction was to lash out, smack hands. Instead, I carefully enfolded Georgie's little fingers in my hands. "Hey, there. Careful, that's attached."

Cecelia leaned back against the changing table. I could see her quickened pulse in her neck, and her breasts heaved with her rapid breathing. "See, you can be taught." She giggled nervously.

I much preferred her giggle to her scowl.

8

CECELIA

I sat on the floor with a movie on the television. I really wished I had a bigger table that would let me spread my scrapbooking supplies out. I needed to see what I had and be able to get at it as I updated and decorated my planner.

I lived by my planner. It helped me get through classes and make sure I never missed an exam. I still loved my planner. It held all my personal organizational notes, like when payday was and when I would have enough money to pay my bills. I also kept little notes like when I thought Sterling Alexander was going to kiss me in it.

That was for me. That wasn't document-document-document so I could build a case against him for a hostile work environment, or anything like that. No, that note was so that I knew someone like him could be attracted to someone like me.

I leaned over and grabbed a stack of sticker books. I was flipping through a collection of *Girl Boss* and positive affirmation statements when there was a sharp knock on my door.

"The fuck?" I wasn't expecting anyone. "Give me a second!" I called out as I extricated myself from the mess of my crafting session.

The knock sounded again.

"Yeah, yeah, yeah. I said hold on." Breath left my body as I yanked the door open and saw Sterling Alexander standing there looking like a super spy.

He was fine, and it took every ounce of my professional demeanor to not be distracted by how attractive that man was every time I stood in his downtown luxury penthouse apartment. I suspected he owned the apartment, and more than likely, the building. But I wasn't at work right now, and he was in a tuxedo.

I swallowed hard and tried to talk.

"Good, you're home." He swept inside with a car seat carrier in his hands. Georgie was wide-eyed and looking around. She had a stuffed ducky she chewed on. Good, he had gotten her at least one toy.

"Mr. Alexander," I managed to croak out. "What are you doing here?"

"You need to watch Georgie." He continued into my small space and looked around him. "This place is a mess. How are you supposed to watch her? You left scissors on the floor, and you have the nerve to be critical of my house?"

He placed the car seat on the floor in the middle of the living room. "Do you have something you can feed her?" He pulled a billfold from his inner jacket packet.

I kept blinking in stunned shock. The man looked like some model for bridal fashions or something in his formal tux, and he kept talking as if I knew what was happening.

He began peeling bills from the stack in his wallet. Holding out a handful of bills toward me, he shook his fist. With his other hand, he reached forward and grasped my hand. It felt like a thousand bolts of electricity pricked my skin. He placed the money into my hand.

"You should be able to have something delivered. You don't have diapers here, do you?" He scanned the area around Georgie's car seat.

It was covered in stickers, paper punches, glue sticks, and washi tape, but no diapers, no bottles.

"Ah, I left the diaper bag in the limo. I'll be right back."

He left.

Georgie made a happy giggling sound, and I looked at her. She smiled at me. It was good to see her happy. I guess things were improving at their home.

Sterling walked right back in, as if he had every right to come and go from my apartment as he pleased.

"Diaper bag," he announced as he placed the bag next to the car seat.

"What are you doing here?" I finally came to my senses.

"You need to—"

"You said that, but that doesn't answer my question." I stared at him, my professional demeanor back with a vengeance. I completely separated his overt attractiveness from his being my client. I had stopped staring at him as an attractive man and started staring at him as a client who should not be here.

"I have an event this evening. You need to watch Georgie. That's your job, isn't it?"

I blew out a long puff of air and shook my head with large sweeps of motion that almost made me dizzy. "How many times have I told you I'm not a nanny?"

"Yes, I know. But when I called your agency about sending over a nanny to watch Georgie, they told me I needed to be in contact with you."

"Mr. Alexander, Sterling, my place of work is closed. It has been for hours. If you called them, why am I just now hearing about this?"

"I don't have time, Cecelia. Watch the baby. I will be back late. I'm already late as it is."

He turned to leave.

"Where are you going?" I demanded.

He turned and it looked like he was considering what I said, clueing in that he couldn't simply drop Georgie off at my apartment.

"Right." He reached into the inner pocket and pulled out a folded-up postcard and handed it to me. "This has the information on it."

Reluctantly, I took the postcard. It was red and gold, and before I had a chance to read anything on it, Sterling stepped out of my apartment and closed the door behind him.

The entitlement… the arrogant… How dare he? I dropped the postcard and ran out the door after him. The concrete outside was rough on my bare feet. I dashed down the stairs and did my best to get across the parking area to where he stood next to a waiting limo.

He was unbuttoning his jacket and laughing. I could see someone inside the car waiting for him. He slid into the car.

"Wait!" I yelled as he leaned out to grab the door handle.

He paused and looked at me.

I stared at him and at the woman he was sitting next to. She was stunning, lots of expensive jewelry, smoky makeup, and a designer red dress. My gut clenched. I was going to have to put a sticker over my little memory note that this man had tried to kiss me. That was a memory clearly best forgotten.

"Did she just leave the baby alone?" the woman asked.

"She's in a car seat, she's not going anywhere. And right now, neither should you," I snarled.

"We can talk about this later, Cecelia. I'm expected, and we are late," Sterling chastised me.

"We can talk about this now," I said. "How did you even find out where I live?"

"Go back inside, Cecelia. I will compensate you for your time."

"Seriously? You think this is about money? Sterling, you simply cannot just show up and expect me to be able to watch Georgie because you have a party to go to."

"It's not a party. Go back inside. I don't have time for this."

He pulled the door closed. I had to jump back before my fingers got closed in the door or the limo ran over my toes.

"What the actual hell?" I yelled after him as they drove off.

I picked my way across the parking lot, tiny rocks biting into the bottoms of my feet as I hobbled along. I can't believe the arrogance of that man to just drop Georgie off. As if I were set up to take care of his kid. Was this some kind of retribution because the agency I worked for basically did that to him when they dropped her off?

"What the heck, kid?" I asked the baby when I got back inside. She complained and kicked. I didn't blame her. I wouldn't want to be restrained in a car seat either.

I cast my gaze around my mess. It wasn't safe to take her out. And she shouldn't be here, anyway. It wasn't like he had called me and planned for me to babysit. I wasn't supposed to do things like that, but honestly, if he had asked, I would have. But this? This wasn't right.

With a huff and a growl, I started to gather up my supplies. "I need to make it so you won't get into anything," I said to Georgie.

She started to fuss more, and then she made a face, and... I sighed. She needed a diaper change. I picked up the diaper bag and started to sort through it. Everything was new and still wrapped in plastic and in the original container. I got the impression this was one of those pre-stocked diaper bags. It had everything a diaper bag should have, including diapers. The first one I pulled out was for an infant. It was far too small for Georgie.

I kept rummaging and pulling out more diapers. There was a small collection of diapers in different sizes. Finding one I figured would fit her, I got everything set up before I released Georgie from the car seat.

"Okay, sweetie, it's time for new pants. And then I think we're gonna have to go find out what Uncle Sterling thinks he's getting away with. My time may not seem important to him, but it's my time. And as adorable as you are, you are not my responsibility. It's not that I don't want to spend the evening playing with you. I have plans, boring, lonely plans with stickers and my date book, and there was going to be wine and ice cream later. It's more about setting boundaries. Just because your uncle is hot, and rich, it doesn't mean he can get away with this."

She cooed.

I took it as an agreement.

9

STERLING

"I'll be right back," I said to Katherine, my date for the evening. I left her chatting with Maurice Hunt to go in search of more champagne. Maurice had cornered me early, making sure to secure a financial pledge from the Alexander estate. Only I hadn't agreed to anything yet. There was a game that needed to be played. Rules of engagement, as it were. There was a certain level of conversation to be had, maybe even a presentation to sit through. It seemed like a buzzkill to whip the checkbook out and make my contribution before all of the festivities even happened. Fortunately, tonight, there wasn't a stage with a podium for speeches. Tonight was all about chit-chat and networking.

Katherine smiled and let her hand trail down my arm before grasping my fingers and squeezing. So far this evening, other than the confusion and mild unpleasantness surrounding having Cecelia watch Georgie, I was having a great time. Katherine made it abundantly clear that she anticipated returning home with me when we were done here.

Could I leave Georgie with Cecelia all night? I didn't think that was going to be an option. After all, Cecelia had not seemed onboard with the whole idea, anyway. So, speeding this evening along seemed like a good idea. That way, I could still show off my dance skills and spin Katherine across the floor, get her back home for a proper seduction, and return to Cecelia's in time to pick up Georgie before midnight.

There was a bit of a commotion off to my left, but someone always got a little drunk at these things. Especially if they had a private happy hour in their limo on the way over. Having big money didn't always mean people knew how to behave appropriately. As if the money excused piss-poor decisions, like arriving at a charity ball buzzed. This was supposed to be a classy event, a fundraiser for friends of the children's museum. And as such, those of us with deep pockets were invited.

Ignoring the commotion, I sauntered back to Maurice and Katherine, intending to make a financial promise that would either turn Maurice into my best friend for the rest of the evening or get him off my back. I hoped for the latter.

'What's going on over there?" Katherine asked as I held up the glass I brought back for her.

I glimpsed over my shoulder and shrugged. I didn't know and I wasn't particularly interested.

Just then, a couple of loud women walked past us chittering about someone's baby mama and how young women of this current generation have no sense of decorum. I shook my head. If there was a baby-mama situation going on, it probably had more to do with the lies the poor girl had bought than anything else. Probably, some guy made promises and forgot to tell his wife about getting his side piece pregnant, or he failed to make child support payments. Either way, it wasn't something I intended on giving my attention to.

I was here to contribute and enjoy myself while doing so. Gossip wasn't my thing.

Katherine's fingers bit into my arm. "Sterling," she hissed out my name through clenched teeth.

"Katherine, what's the matter? Are you all right?"

"It's that woman," she said. Her hand tightened on my arm.

"What woman?" I twisted to look back at the area where the commotion was going on. Cecelia was storming toward me with Georgie in her car seat carrier hanging in her hand. "Crap."

"You said she was your nanny. She is not acting like a nanny, Sterling. Is there something you need to tell me?"

I didn't like the tone in her voice. She was accusing me of not being truthful. I didn't like that very much, especially after she had already joked about the situation seeming a little too strange to be real.

I let out a long breath. "I'm not sure what you are insinuating, and I do not know why she is here. Excuse me," I said. I adjusted my jacket and walked toward Cecelia. Whatever she thought was doing, it needed to stop right now.

"You need to leave," I said as I approached her.

She stopped on the edge of the space between the tables and the dance floor. She glared at me and lifted the car seat out to me.

"Take Georgie and go home. We will discuss this later."

"No, Mr. Alexander, we will not. We can talk about it right now in front of everybody, or—"

I took the car seat in one hand and wrapped my other hand around Cecelia's arm. I moved her out of the center of the event and toward the back wall. We were not going to do any of this with an audience.

"Get your hands off me." Cecelia writhed in my grasp. She was soft, and my fingers bit into her arm deeper. "You're hurting me."

I released my hold of her. My intention wasn't to hurt her, just to move her.

"What are you doing here?" I asked. "I said I would be back later."

"I don't know what you think my job is, Mr. Alexander, but I am not Georgie's babysitter or her nanny. You overstepped."

"I overstepped. My bad. I am kind of in the middle of something here. So, will you take Georgie back? I'll give you the key to the penthouse. You can take her there where all of her toys are, and we can discuss this when I get back."

"You keep saying that, but I don't think you are actually listening to anything I am saying."

"Sterling, do you want to tell me what's really going on here?" Katherine joined us, a strained expression on her face.

I was not going to be pleased if Cecelia's little stunt got in the way of my plans.

"Is it true, what I keep hearing? You're the baby's mother?" Katherine asked.

Cecelia let a rather unladylike snort out of her nose. "What? Are you kidding me?"

"Katherine." I tried to keep my voice down. "I told you, she is from the agency."

"I am not Georgie's mother. Didn't he tell you about the baby in the limo? I mean, you were there when he abandoned her with me."

I turned and glared at Cecelia. "I did not abandon Georgie with you. I left her with you to watch for the evening."

"That is not something I agreed to, therefore, child abandonment," Cecelia snapped back.

"Why is she here, then?" Katherine asked.

"I'm here because Sterling thinks he can do whatever he wants. And I am not some flunky he can order about."

Katherine looked at Cecelia while she spoke. A sneer marred her lovely face as if she were looking at something distasteful. I tried to see what she saw when she looked at Cecelia. Only, I didn't see someone worth grimacing at.

Cecelia's clothing, while perfectly reasonable at any other time, was not appropriate right here or right now, like a zit on a beauty queen's forehead the day of the competition. Her jeans showed off her curves, and her shirt was a bit too tight across her chest. I thought she looked delightful.

Katherine obviously thought otherwise. She turned to me before speaking. "You need to get your employee taken care of. I don't really care what you have to do, but this is embarrassing."

"I don't work for him," Cecelia snapped.

Katherine barely glanced at Cecelia before locking her eyes with mine. "Take care of this, Sterling, and get rid of the kid, or I'll be calling a car to take me home."

I narrowed my gaze at Katherine. I didn't like how she was behaving toward Cecelia. I wasn't a fan of Cecelia's being there, but she was, and I had to deal with it. Katherine's idle threat on top of everything else was poorly timed. Right at that moment, I wasn't focused on whether I'd see her red dress on my floor tonight. I was a bit more concerned with how to rectify the situation I was now forced to deal with.

"Don't do that, Katherine. Calling a car isn't necessary," I said evenly.

"Good." She crossed her arms and looked down her nose at Cecelia and at me as if she expected us to perform for her.

I carefully set Georgie's car seat on the floor. It was the first time I noticed the baby was blissfully asleep. At least one of us was unfazed by everything going on.

"Cecelia, please, take the baby back. I'm on a date and I need you to watch Georgie for me."

"I can't," Cecelia started. "Maybe if you had spoken to me earlier about this—"

"Yes, you can. And you will." Katherine picked up the car seat and shoved it at Cecelia. The action was rough and jerky.

Georgie started crying.

"See what you have done? The brat is crying, and you need to leave. Take her and go," Katherine said.

I didn't like seeing Georgie in distress, especially when she had nothing to do with any of this.

"Katherine," I growled.

Cecelia had placed the car seat back on the floor and knelt down next to it, trying to comfort Georgie.

"Is everything okay over here?" Robin Johnson, Maurice's co-chair of the event, calmly joined us as if we were simply chatting about the weather.

10

CECELIA

I was there to make a point, and as long as everyone talked over me and didn't listen to anything I said, the point was lost. Georgie was upset, and I was the only one who seemed to care about her at all. Maybe this hadn't been one of my smarter moves.

Sterling's date was a nasty piece of snobbery. But then again, I was a non-entity to someone like her. I was a member of the working population and below her consideration. Whatever. I did not need her getting in the middle of my attempt at having a conversation with Sterling. And I really didn't need her upsetting the baby.

I unstrapped Georgie and lifted her out of the car seat. I did my best to soothe her. While I was taking care of the baby, an older lady came over and started talking in hushed tones. My attempt at getting Sterling to understand that he couldn't dump Georgie on me would never be properly made.

From the initial look of triumph on his date's face, I figured I would be kicked out of the event in a moment.

The older lady turned a smiling face to me. The date scrunched up her face and pulled her pursed lips back and actually snarled. I wasn't certain what was going on. Georgie sniffled and settled, but she was wide awake now and looking at all the bright lights and colors that were around us.

"Are you serious?" the date said. "That's it, I'm calling a car."

"Katherine, don't call a car," Sterling said. He sounded exhausted.

"I don't think you can say anything to me that will change my mind about leaving."

Sterling shook his head slowly. "I'm not trying to change your mind. Don't call for a car. Take the limo."

"Wha—" Her voice was shrill at first before she lowered it to a whisper. "What do you think is going to happen here, Sterling? This evening has been ruined."

He nodded. "Yes, I know. Take the limo. I'll get a car. You shouldn't be put out anymore."

"Don't think this means you can call me after this," she said before she turned with a dramatic flip of her hair and stormed off.

"What a darling little girl," the older woman said as if the drama of the moment before hadn't happened right in front of her. She held her hands out to take the baby. "May I?"

I handed Georgie over.

"I haven't held a baby since my grandchildren were little. She is so precious," she cooed over Georgie. "What's her name?"

"Her name is Georgie," I answered before Sterling had a chance to.

"I didn't know you had a baby," she continued to coo in the same tone of voice. People always talked crazily around babies. I wasn't any different.

Sterling cleared his throat. "She's not mine."

The older woman stopped her bouncing from side to side and leveled a neutral stare at Sterling. I recognized a disapproving glare when I saw one.

"She's my late sister's child. I only have temporary custody. Robin, I do apologize for what happened," Sterling started.

"I think the two of you need to talk without any additional interruptions. I will take Georgie here, and you go dance and talk."

Robin swirled away with Georgie in her arms.

"Fine," I said as Sterling grabbed my arm again.

He placed his arm around my back and began a slow, turning dance. It took me a moment to realize he was waltzing with me. Once I realized what we were doing, I stopped fumbling over my feet and began to dance.

"You ruined my date," he said with a stern tone.

Being this close to him, even with him upset like this and my being angry at him, it still confused my body. I shouldn't have felt butterflies in my middle, and my pulse shouldn't have been racing.

"While I had no intentions of ruining your date, I needed to get my point across. It's not my fault you dropped Georgie off unannounced or that your date wasn't understanding."

"What was I supposed to do with her?" Sterling asked.

"I don't know, she was your date."

"I mean the baby," he grumbled.

"Come on, Sterling, you are a smart man. You wouldn't be where you are today if you weren't. And I'm sure your butler, assistant, Wayne, is also a smart man. Somehow, I think if the two of you had put any thought into the situation, you could have figured something out."

"I called the agency," Sterling said.

He was a good dancer. I kind of hated it. Moving so smoothly across the floor in his arms should not have felt this nice. But it did, and I liked it entirely too much. We were so close together, it was hard to keep eye contact. I kept staring at his mouth.

"I don't work for some kind of staffing agency."

"They told me that you would help me out. That I should ask you," he said.

I sighed. He didn't want to do the hard work, so he took that to mean that I would babysit. "They didn't mean I would watch Georgie. They meant, ask me how to find childcare. How did you find out where I live, anyway? Did the office tell you?"

If someone at work told him where I lived, I was going to pitch a fit. That was information that they should not be giving out.

"I was running out of time," he practically snarled. "Wayne did a reverse look up or something. He got your address off the internet."

"Look, I get it, taking care of Georgie is more complicated than you expected. But taking shortcuts that interfere with other people, that interfere with my life, isn't going to help. Maybe I would have been available to help out tonight if you'd asked. But you didn't. You can't do that to me. I will not put up with it. Georgie is your responsibility, not mine."

"I overstepped," he admitted.

"Thank you for saying that." We were both quiet for a long time after that. The wind was sucked out of my indignant sails. Saying he'd overstepped was a gross understatement. I would never get an apology out of a man like Sterling Alexander. An admission of action was the best I was going to get.

He tightened his arms around me, and I rested my head on his shoulder. This was far too comfortable, far too exhilarating.

"Having Georgie in my life has been more challenging than I could have anticipated."

I didn't say anything, letting him talk.

"I wasn't prepared. Nothing could have prepared me for learning of Argene's death. She was so young and vibrant. She was so much younger than me. I had no idea that she had a child. I'm only willing to admit I don't know what I'm doing because it's completely obvious."

His words were low, soft murmurs against my cheek. I wanted to lean into him. Anything to get closer and let those whispers of breath become flutters of his lips against my skin. I couldn't, shouldn't be thinking these thoughts I was having about him and his lips and my body. I needed to be professional.

"I know having Georgie is hard. If it's too much, you need to let me know. Ideally, she should stay with you, but if you cannot, are not capable of caring for her, you need to tell me. Think about it over the weekend. We can find a foster situation for her until her bio-father is located."

"What happens if he isn't located?" His voice was rough.

"She'll be placed with an adoption agency. It's not what her mother wanted, but if that's what's best for the child, that's what we need to do."

He stopped dancing and glowered at me. His arms caged me in. "No."

"Trust me, it's better that she be raised by people who want her around, and not someone who considers her a chore." I pushed out of his embrace and looked around to see if I could find the woman with Georgie. They were sitting at a table. Georgie had the woman's earring half in her mouth, half in her fists. The woman smiled and had all of her attention on the baby. They were fine.

I put my hand on Sterling's chest. He wrapped his warm hand over my fingers, and I felt that touch in my core somehow. My throat went dry. This whole situation was hard.

"Good night, Sterling. I'll see you in a few days. We have another appointment, unless you want me to have someone else assigned to your case."

"No." His thumb skimmed back and forth over the back of my hand. "I don't need someone else assigned to my case. I'll see you."

I walked away. When I crashed into the party earlier, it was so obvious to me that's what I had to do. But this felt wrong. Leaving him like that seemed wrong. I stopped at the valet desk on my way out.

"Could you please call a car for Mr. Alexander? He'll be leaving soon," I asked as I handed over the ticket for my car.

I took one of the many twenty dollar bills out of my pocket and waited.

"Thanks." I handed over the tip as the valet held my door open for me. I looked back over my shoulder, seeing if I could get one last glimpse of Sterling in a tux before I left. I didn't see him. There were too many people between us.

11

STERLING

As I stood there in the middle of the dance floor with couples swaying around me, watching Cecelia walk away, I became aware of several things all at once.

Failure was not an option, and I was currently failing Georgie. I was failing the memory and trust of my sister. Argene had wanted me to take care of Georgie. Me. I had been named. It was not some throw-away line in a request to send her to family but a specific request that I be the one to take Georgie should anything happen to Argene and the father not be located.

But Georgie's father's name wasn't provided. Was Argene keeping Georgie from him? Did I need to protect the child from her other family? I couldn't protect her if she was put into foster care.

I wasn't going to let that happen.

I watched every swaying step of Cecelia's hips until she was obscured from view. I hadn't even glimpsed at Katherine as she had left the party. I wasn't even disappointed that Katherine was no longer coming home with me or even an option for future potential interactions. But I felt a sense of loss with Cecelia gone.

Quickly scanning the event, I located Robin and Georgie and strode over to them.

"Did you find a resolution for your little love triangle?" she asked as I stepped up to the table. She tilted her head, and I took the seat next to her.

"Hardly a love triangle. I messed up."

Robin took her attention away from Georgie to give me a perplexed look. "Beg pardon? Did Sterling Alexander just admit to not being perfect?"

I laughed, tension rushing away from my shoulders. Robin Johnson knew me better than I had clearly given her credit for.

"You're a natural at this," I said as I pointed to her and Georgie.

"I've had children, and grandchildren. And I raised my children. I didn't have nannies around the clock. I learned. You can learn too. I am sorry to learn of your sister's passing."

"You knew Argene?" I asked.

"Not exactly. But I had met her a time or two, back when your mother was still with us."

Robin was old money, old family. And she knew my parents, and by extension, we were friendly enough. Enough that I felt comfortable asking advice.

"How am I supposed to learn?" I eased back in the chair and stretched my legs out under the table. Georgie seemed content. She did when she was with other people.

"Hmm," Robin hummed. She seemed to be thinking. "Well, I had help. My mother, my grandmother, and pretty much anyone who thought I was doing something wrong."

I shrugged. "Unfortunately, my mother is no longer with us. But even if she were, she didn't think that men raised children. That was the woman's role in the family."

"Well, your parents were from an older generation. Times have changed. Who was that young woman? The one who brought Georgie in this evening."

"She's my case worker," I said flatly. At least I thought she was still my case worker.

Robin nodded. "Ah, I think I see. You need to get into some parenting classes."

"Do they exist? I have some books."

Georgie yawned and rubbed her tiny fists into her eyes.

"You need to take this adorable baby home while she is still adorable and not fussing. Monday morning, call Maurice's office and talk to his assistant. She'll be able to find some classes for you."

I raised my brows at her in an unasked question.

"The children's museum is all about education and outreach. She has the resources to find what you need. Call." Robin picked Georgie up with her as she stood.

She pressed her lips against the baby's hair and murmured as I got the car seat ready. She kissed Georgie one last time before placing her into the car seat. As I buckled Georgie in, Robin grabbed my arm and squeezed. A car waited for us when I stepped outside. She fell asleep on the ride home.

I had an entire weekend on my own with the baby. Wayne prepared meals, but I still was the one to feed and change the baby.

It was as if some switch got flipped to the *On* position inside. I was somehow better attuned to Georgie's needs. I could interpret her signals better. I wasn't about to get her a cat, but I did order a stuffed cat toy.

When the toy arrived and I gave it to her, her entire body shook as she laughed and squirmed. She hugged the toy in her little arms and bit down on one of the ears. She was happy and no longer stressed out because I didn't know what I was doing.

I still didn't know what I was doing, but I had a hint more experience with her. And I was not going to let that child down.

It was a long couple of days before Monday arrived. I needed to call Maurice's assistant, and I needed Cecelia to come over for our appointment. I wasn't used to having to wait for people. If I was ready to start a project, I tended to jump in and get started no matter the time of day or night. Georgia wasn't a tech problem I needed to find a solution for. I had to wait for the people and resources that were going to help me.

I couldn't say that mornings had settled into a routine that we had all mastered. But it wasn't nearly the struggle as it had been even four days earlier. And there were fewer tears involved. I had Georgie in her highchair. Wayne had tepid oatmeal ready for her, and I had a hot cup of coffee. I wasn't dressed for the day, Georgie only had on a diaper, but we were doing it. We were figuring this out.

The concierge pinged, and a moment later, Wayne announced, "Miss Cecelia is on her way up. Do you want to take a moment to prepare for your guest?"

I shook my head. I didn't care if Cecelia saw me in sweats and a T-shirt. This wasn't a social call, and I wasn't trying to impress her. I continued to spoon mush into Georgie's mouth, and she managed to get it everywhere.

"Miss Cecelia, Mr. Sterling." Wayne introduced her as he led her into the kitchen.

"You're early," I said. "Want coffee?"

"Thank you," Cecelia said as she took a seat. She looked severe this morning. She wore a gray suit with a plain pink shirt. Her hair was twisted at the back of her head. She really was a lovely woman, even dressed for business. "Did you think about what I mentioned the other night?"

She thought she was here to take Georgie into foster care. That wasn't happening.

"I did. I had a conversation with Robin Johnson after you left."

Cecelia furrowed her brow.

"The woman who swept in like a grandmother. She gave me some guidance."

"You take guidance?" Cecelia's voice was sharp.

"Cute." I acknowledged her sarcasm by raising my own brows. "I take guidance. I purchased everything you told me to. And believe it or not, I even know how to ask for help. Which I am doing right now. The books you suggested have some good information, but they do not really help with the hands-on aspect of this. And as you can see, Georgie is a hands-on kind of girl."

She had a fist full of mush and was trying to chew on her hand.

"I understand there are parenting courses. I need some assistance in locating those, getting signed up. Also, I am going to need a little more coaching through the day-to-day."

Cecelia stared at me for a long moment.

"Your coffee, Miss." Wayne placed a mug in front of Cecelia.

Her gaze fell to the mug, and she stared at it for even longer. "What made you decide to keep her?" Cecelia's voice was quiet.

"Not keeping Georgie isn't really an option. She's family, and it isn't her fault that I don't know how to take care of her. But I'm the adult here, and it is my responsibility. She is my sister's daughter. I owe it to both of them, Georgie and Argene, to do my best. She stays with me until her father is located."

Cecelia lifted her eyes to meet mine. Tears pooled against her lower lids, and her lip quivered.

She blinked a few times before wiping her face. "I'm really happy to hear that."

I reached out and placed her hand over mine. Warmth spread up my arm. She started to laugh in relief. "I'm really glad you are keeping her. I'd miss her."

The way Cecelia's gaze was locked with mine, and the warmth that flowed between us where our hands touched, it felt as if she were saying she'd miss me. Maybe that was just my ego talking.

12

CECELIA

Sterling didn't have a clue how to parent a child, but that didn't make him a bad person. I needed to shift my judgmental attitude. I was making moral assessments when they weren't appropriate because of my past. The man needed an education, and part of my job to make their family function was to help him with that education.

Instead, I spent my first week being pissed off that someone thought handing a baby off to a man like him was a good idea. But if they hadn't, I wouldn't be going out with him and Georgie. Today was training day. I had no idea how to train him to be a parent. So, I was showing him what I thought I would do if I had a kid.

The elevator door slid open. As usual, Wayne was waiting to escort me inside. "Good morning, Miss Cecelia."

"Good morning, Wayne. Is everyone ready?"

"By everyone, you mean Mr. Sterling and Miss Georgie. They are still making their preparations."

"You aren't coming with us?" My insides clenched a little. Was I nervous he would say yes, or no?

"Who, me? Certainly not. My duties keep me here."

I swear I saw him shiver as if going to the zoo was distasteful. He led me into the living room. A few days ago, there was no way to tell a child lived here. Now, there was no way to miss it. Foam pool noodles were cut to size and wrapped over corners of tables and walls. A few soft toys were scattered about. A pink checkerboard quilt was spread out on the floor. Georgie sat in the middle surrounded by fabric cubes and a few stuffed animals. She wore a cotton onesie with a yellow sundress over that. A matching bucket hat was already on her head and a bow was tied under her chin to keep it in place.

I was also wearing yellow. We almost matched, only I didn't have a bucket hat with a strap tied under my chin.

Sterling was down on the floor next to her. He was not ready, still in the plaid soft pants and T-shirt I assumed he'd slept in. I made sure to keep my eyes on his face or my attention on the baby. While she looked content to play on her blanket, he did not look happy as he wrestled with a collection of grey and black tubes. At first, I thought it might be a vacuum cleaner, but when I saw the wheels, I figured it was a stroller.

"I thought those things came already assembled," I said as I put my tote bag down and lifted Georgie. "Uh, you're gaining weight."

"She's a baby. Don't fat shame her," Sterling grumbled.

I laughed. "I'm hardly fat shaming her. Babies are supposed to be pudgy. It's a good thing she's gaining weight. It means you are feeding her." I sat and put her on my knee and began bouncing my foot.

"I think I'm feeding her," Sterling said. He didn't look up from his task. "But I can't tell if anything is getting inside. There is more food all over her and the highchair and the floor than we ever start with."

"Well, whatever you are doing, at least it's working. So, what's going on here?" I asked.

"Some assembly required." Sterling reached out and smacked a large box with an image of a stroller on it. "They lie. It's all assembly."

"I normally wouldn't recommend spending more money, but why don't you toss all of that back into the box, and we go to a baby store and buy something already put together?" I suggested.

He looked up at me and tilted his head slightly to the side. "I thought that company went out of business?"

"Oh, yeah, the big chain store did. But there's got to be a local one we can go to."

"I usually just order online. That's how I got everything else. Well, except for the highchair. That came from a big box store, and it did require assembly."

I lifted Georgie from my knee and put her back on the quilt. With a sigh, I pulled out my phone and started searching for baby supply stores in the city. I found one that looked promising.

I hit their phone number and waited until someone picked up the phone.

"Hi, do y'all carry strollers, or are you just clothes?" I asked as soon as the person on the other end of the line finished their spiel.

"No, I'm sorry. We're a clothing boutique. We have some toys. Have you tried Hand Me Downs? They usually have strollers."

I called the recommended place, and the lady who worked there assured me they had several strollers in stock.

"Okay," I told Sterling. "We can go to this shop, Hand Me Downs, and pick up a stroller. Even if it isn't exactly what you want, it will get you through a few days until either you figure how to get this one together, or—"

"Or I order something else. Sounds like a plan." He finished dropping the pieces into the box. "I need to wash up. Wayne should have Georgie's snacks and a couple of bottles ready and packed for us."

I picked the baby up. "I'll get her changed and in the car seat. Meet you back here?"

Sterling stepped in close and put his hand on my arm. We gazed at each other for a moment. My insides twisted as he leaned down and placed a kiss on top of Georgie's hat.

I held my breath until he walked away. Oh, boy, that had been close. I wish it had been closer. The twists and turns in my middle were definitely excited for a day alone with him and the baby.

I was putting Georgie into the car seat after a fresh change.

Wayne set an insulated lunch bag next to me. "Miss Georgie's bottles. There's also some applesauce and these little dissolvable cookie treats she seems to like."

"Thank you."

"I will let Mr. Sterling know the car is ready. Have a pleasant day, Miss Cecelia." He left before I had a chance to tell him the same.

"Ready?" I looked up when Sterling came back.

He was crazy handsome. He looked like a movie super spy in a tux. For the day-to-day clothes I'd seen him in, he tended toward business basics, dress slacks and button-downs, and he looked super good in those. His sleepwear… I don't know what miracle occurred that he now wore his sleepwear when I showed up, but… tight T-shirts showed off the exceptional muscles in his arms and shoulders. He had firm, square pecs, and if the shirts weren't a little loose around the middle, I would be able to confirm whether he had a six-pack.

It wasn't professional of me to ogle the man. But it was really difficult to not notice the package he had between his legs. The soft pants he slept in didn't hide a whole lot. They also hung a little low on his hips.

Those pants and T-shirts were the equivalent of sexy underwear as far as I was concerned.

I thought if I could behave while he was cavorting about in his sexy sleepwear, I could handle seeing Sterling in anything. I was wrong. My throat went dry and I forgot what I was about to say. I made a croaking sound back in my throat.

"Cecelia, are you okay?"

I nodded and tried to clear my throat as I stood. Jeans. Sterling Alexander in jeans would be my downfall. He wore a T-shirt he must have picked up while on vacation in the islands, and those jeans fit him like they were made for him, and then he lived in them, so they conformed to the shape and swell of his thighs and butt. He didn't look like some super-rich tech guy. He looked like an underwear model.

He grabbed the handle to the car seat and picked up Georgie. I hitched my tote bag onto my shoulder and picked up the lunch bag with Georgie's food.

The elevator slid open, and I got in after him. I was in an elevator right next to probably the single most handsome man in the world and his niece. And we looked like a family. Both Georgie and I were in yellow dresses, and Sterling's Grand Cayman shirt was also yellow.

It wasn't until he was strapping Georgie's car seat into the back of the limo that it occurred to me that I could have pointed out his yellow shirt and given him the opportunity to change. But the butterflies in my middle loved how we looked like we belonged together.

"This looks like a used clothing store," Sterling said as the limo pulled up in front of the store.

"It probably is," I said. "It's called Hand Me Downs."

Sterling's brow furrowed and his expression darkened. "I can afford a new stroller."

"Look, you can be a total snob and refuse to buy a used stroller to use for one day, and we can spend the rest of the morning driving around Dallas looking for a stroller. Or we can go inside and find something that will work for going to the zoo. I know you can afford something very high-end. That stroller is in parts in your living room right now."

13

STERLING

"Hey, y'all, what can I help you with this morning?" The salesclerk greeted us with enthusiasm.

After the dressing down Cecelia gave me, I followed her inside the store. She was right, there was nothing wrong with buying a used stroller to get us through today. She tended to be right, and she wasn't afraid to put me in my place.

Her spunk was refreshing in a world of women trying to appeal to my better nature by agreeing to everything I said. I had a few colleagues who wouldn't just do what I said because I said it. But for the most part, no one challenged me the way she did.

"We need a stroller. We ordered one and it showed up needing to be put together. Until that can happen..." Cecelia told the sales lady.

"Let me show you what we have in stock. Now if that fancy stroller you have at home continues to give you fits—"

"How do you know it's fancy?" I asked.

"Oh, it's always the fancy ones. I swear, the more they cost, the more DIY they require. Anyway, we do offer an assembly service. Now, is this just for this sleeping beauty?" She continued until we were in a row of strollers.

The quantity and variety were a little staggering.

"Only one," Cecelia said.

"They have strollers for more than one?" I asked.

"Of course. We have strollers for multiple infants, and for infant-toddler combos. You want something you can lock that car seat into?"

"Yes, please."

We left with a stroller that was more a frame to convert the car seat than an old-fashioned pram. There was an under-carriage storage area that Cecelia insisted on. We were in and out of the store in a matter of minutes.

"Why don't you have Wayne gather all the parts up to the other stroller and get it delivered here for them to put together?" Cecelia suggested as we continued on toward the zoo.

When she suggested the zoo, I hadn't realized it was a haven for mothers and babies. Cecelia and Georgie looked like they belonged. I stuck out like a sore thumb.

"Did you know it was like this?" I asked as we waited in the line for entry tickets.

"Crowded? I thought it would be empty on a weekday."

"I meant all the mothers and kids." I spoke low so that I wasn't overheard.

"Kids love animals. It seems like a natural fit to come here."

I paid for the tickets, and we followed the flow of the crowd into the park.

"Is everything I do with Georgie going to be overwhelmingly mothers and their kids?"

Cecelia smiled at me and laughed a bit. "Probably. I'm sure there are 'daddy and me' groups you could join, but—"

"Daddy and me?"

"Groups for dads who are the primary caregiver in the family. A lot of early development classes are called 'mommy and me'. You could go, but as you already mentioned, lots of moms."

I muttered about the term 'daddy and me'. Cecelia kept glancing at me and laughing.

"That makes you really uncomfortable, doesn't it?"

I let out a low grumble. We were still in a big crowd of moms and strollers. I leaned in close, my lips almost brushing Cecelia's ear. "My last date called me 'Daddy'. I'd be more comfortable if you were the one calling me Daddy and not some child, if you understand what I'm saying."

The blush started on Cecelia's cheeks and then spread over all of her exposed skin. It was a charming look on her. I would have to remember that.

Her eyes went wide, and she smiled but then stared hard at the ground. "Sterling," she said through clenched teeth.

That's all she said, my name, and then she kept blushing. Yeah, she could call me Daddy anytime.

"So, where are we headed?" I asked as if she weren't lit up like a beacon and my jeans weren't getting tight in the crotch.

She cleared her throat. "I'm not sure. I'm just following the crowd."

The tide of zoo visitors pulled us along until we entered a petting zoo area. Strollers were lined up like motorcycles at a roadhouse bar. Toddlers scrambled everywhere.

"Is this what I have to look forward to?" I muttered out loud.

"If you still have custody of Georgie when she's walking, then yeah, probably."

I grabbed the stroller away from Cecelia and kept walking. I didn't want to be overwhelmed by all the kids. They outnumbered the adults, and I didn't want them to overwhelm us. I navigated back to the flamingo display before I lifted Georgie out of the stroller and held her so she could look at the pink birds.

"Hey, look at me," Cecelia said.

I turned. She had her camera phone pointed at us. "I thought you might like a picture."

"Come here. You should be in this picture with us." I held out my hand and took the phone from her.

We positioned ourselves, and I held up the phone for a selfie.

"Oh, we should get the flamingoes behind us," Cecelia said.

As we tried to get situated so I could take a picture that also showed the birds in the background, someone's grandmother approached us. "Would you like me to take that for you?"

I handed her the phone. I held Georgie in one arm and wrapped the other around Cecelia, tugging her in tight against me. She felt nice. Like she belonged tucked in against me.

"What a lovely family. This is going to make a great picture," the lady cooed as she pointed the camera phone at us.

"Oh, we're—" Cecelia started.

"We're so grateful you could help us out." I cut Cecelia off. That lady did not need to know we were not a family. "Thank you."

I looked at the photo before sharing it with Cecelia. The lady was right. We looked like we belonged.

"Were you going to say anything about how we are all in yellow?" I asked Cecelia. I must have subconsciously picked this shirt so that I coordinated with her and Georgie.

"By the time I realized it, we were already in the car. You aren't mad, are you?"

I shook my head. I actually liked it.

We strolled past enclosures and through exhibits. I carried Georgie for a while before setting her back in the car seat, now stroller. Cecelia carried her for a bit, and after a while, we only picked her up when we reached a new animal to look at. When we reached the tigers, Georgie made the same set of noises that meant cat for her.

"I guess cats really are her favorite," Cecelia said.

"I'm still not getting her a cat," I insisted.

After a snack and a bottle, Georgie grew fussy.

"I'll change her," Cecelia announced. She picked up the diaper bag and headed into the restroom.

I found a bench and waited. I could handle this. This was easy. Take the kid to the zoo, feed her snacks. There was a shack decorated to look like a village hut where I could grab something for Cecelia and me to eat. We'd be through the zoo by lunchtime. Georgie would be exhausted and take her first nap.

My utopian ideas of a blissful zoo outing were shattered when the diaper bag landed in my lap.

"You haven't restocked this. There are no diapers that fit Georgie in there. And there are no changes of clothes," Cecelia snarled with anger.

Georgie, only in a diaper, was sniffling and crying. At least she wasn't howling.

"Some nice lady in the bathroom had an extra diaper I could borrow."

I rummaged in the bag. I hadn't really looked to see what was inside. I pulled out a handful of diapers. "What are these?" I asked. It was a rhetorical question. They were obviously diapers.

"Those are newborn size. Georgie is bigger, and her output quantity is higher," she said.

Diapers come in sizes. Of course they did. But the dress I pulled out next, I knew fit Georgie.

"Clothes."

Cecelia huffed at me. "Look at that, Sterling. It's all scratchy lace and velvet. Do you really want to put her in a hot, miserable velvet dress today? This bag needs to be restocked after every outing. It needs diapers, and it needs at least two full changes of clothes."

I didn't deserve all the anger she was focusing on me. "And I know this how? Cecelia, please, this is why I need your help. To you, it was obvious. I have no idea what goes in a diaper bag."

She pursed her lips and breathed heavily through her nose.

"I'm sorry, you're right." Her voice was clipped, but loud enough for it to be clear that she meant it. "Georgie had a bit of a meltdown, and then there were no diapers that fit. The bag is now completely out of wipes. I felt like I had completely messed everything up. I'm sorry I let my frustration get the better of me."

I stood and placed an arm around her shoulder. She was getting tired, and unlike Georgie, who had ready access to snacks all morning long, Cecelia hadn't had anything to eat or drink since she arrived at the penthouse. "It's okay. We're both learning."

She wiped her eyes. "That wasn't very professional of me. Could you please buy Georgie a T-shirt at the gift kiosk so she's not exposed? There isn't any sunscreen in the bag either, and I don't want her to get a sunburn."

14

CECELIA

I snapped and yelled at Sterling. He was so close when it came to doing the right thing, but then he messed up and hadn't restocked the diaper bag. And part of me felt that was my fault. How was I supposed to do my job objectively when I let his lack of information make me so irritated?

Was I going to be like this for all my future clients, or was Sterling a special case?

It didn't help when he was such a constant flirt. Or that I couldn't resist him.

He tore the tag from the small shirt as he walked back from the gift shop. He handed it to me. It was yellow.

I got Georgie dressed and settled back in the car seat with a bottle.

"Better?" he asked.

I nodded, and he put an arm over my shoulder and pulled me against his chest. He placed a kiss on my temple. "We're both learning. Let's get some lunch. Georgie isn't the only one getting tired."

I nodded. I was disappointed in myself and overwhelmed. He kissed me. It didn't matter that it was a comforting gesture. He kissed me, and my brain short-circuited.

I followed behind as Sterling pushed the stroller back to the front gate. The limo was waiting. Sterling strapped in the car seat, and I folded up the stroller like an umbrella. The driver put the frame in the trunk and handed the other bags inside before holding the door for me to climb in.

"Do you want to stop on the way back, or should I have something delivered?"

I glanced at Georgie. Her lids were heavy. She fought off the nap that was in process of claiming her. A car nap seemed like a good idea. I stretched out on the wide backseat, curling my feet up behind me and resting my head on Sterling's lap. I was too tired to care about professionalism.

"Have something delivered. I'm going to close my eyes. We've got a lot to work on when we get back."

I think I felt Sterling stroke my hair, but I was asleep in moments, lulled there by the movement of the car. I woke up a few moments before the limo pulled in front of Sterling's building.

"Rested?" he asked.

I stretched and sat up. Realization of what I had done dawned on me. I groaned. "I am so sorry, that was so unprofessional. I did not mean to use you as a pillow."

"You're fine. You can use me as your pillow anytime."

I felt a blush burn my cheeks.

I didn't know what to say. Fortunately, the driver stopped the limo, and it was time to unpack Georgie and all of her things and lug it all up to the top floor.

"How was this morning's excursion?" Wayne greeted us as the elevator doors slid open.

"Tiring," Sterling said. He stepped out of the elevator and carried the car seat with the sleeping baby toward her room.

"It was a bit more than we expected." I didn't have to tell him I lost my cool, and that we didn't have a properly packed diaper bag. I handed Wayne the stroller frame. I didn't know where to put it.

"Your lunches have arrived," he said.

I nodded and followed him to the kitchen. I was starving.

Sterling came in and set down a white monitor on the table before he sat.

"When did you get a baby monitor?" I asked.

Sterling shrugged. "It was on your original shopping list. I purchased everything from that list after your initial visit."

I nodded. I was still tired, more mentally weary than physically. The brief nap in the car was refreshing, but I felt so stupid for first having yelled at Sterling and then having used him as a pillow. I shouldn't have done that.

Wayne served lunch and placed our plates in front of us. "Is there anything else I can get for you?"

I nodded. "We're going to need a notepad and a pen, please."

He handed me a lined notepad and a pen moments later.

"Okay," I started. "We need to make some lists."

"You like lists, don't you?" Sterling teased me.

"They are useful. You were able to shop for Georgie because I left you with lists."

He smirked, or was that half-grin more of a smolder? Whatever the expression was he gave me, it was gone a split second later when he put a fork full of food in his mouth.

"What were today's challenges?"

"Don't you mean what we need to fix?" he asked.

I shook my head. "Challenges don't necessarily need to be fixed. You need to learn how to approach the problem so that it's not a problem."

"The stroller."

I wrote down what he said, followed by *local resources*.

Sterling tapped that item. "What do you mean?"

"You can't order everything online. Georgie will sometimes have immediate needs. You should know what's available to you. Do you have a twenty-four-hour pharmacy?"

Sterling's brow twisted, making his eyebrows cock up. "That's a good question. I don't take any prescription meds, so…"

I nodded. "Find out. Maybe Wayne has a resource for you that you aren't aware of. High fevers and ear infections never seem to happen in the middle of the afternoon." I drew an arrow from local resources and wrote down *Pharmacy* and then *Emergency Room*. "Find out if the local ER has a pediatric ward, or which children's hospital is closest."

Sterling ran his hand through his hair and let out a breath. "I thought we were going to write down what needed to go into a diaper bag. I didn't think about needing to take her to the emergency room. Add to your list to find her a pediatrician."

"There's so much to learn and do. It's why even after spending as much time with you as I have, it feels like you're behind. Did I forget to tell you to restock the diaper bag? Yes, but with everything else, did I really need to?"

Sterling shook his head. "You shouldn't have needed to tell me to restock a diaper bag. I should have known better. I should have thought about putting together an emergency plan. I've been reacting to the situation. This morning was really nice. I didn't have to worry about not being prepared." He shrugged. "At least until the diaper bag fiasco."

He put his hand over mine, and every time he did that, it sent zaps of electricity up my arm.

We continued to build the list. It grew and took over multiple pages. Wayne took away the lunch dishes. Georgie woke up, but we kept working on the list.

After hours of brainstorming, Sterling had an emergency plan and a task list that involved calling pediatricians in the morning to find Georgie a doctor. And I had a shopping list of items for the diaper bag and for a pediatric medicine cabinet. There wasn't even baby aspirin in the apartment.

Sterling offered to order everything, but he needed everything immediately. What if tonight was the night Georgie got sick?

I thought about asking him to come with me. Had someone who had grown up as rich as Sterling ever been in a big box store? Did he know what discount shopping was? But Georgie was acting tired. She was a little clingy and hugging her stuffed cat toy. Maybe the zoo had been too much for her?

I wanted to be near the two of them.

That thought was what made me realize I needed to leave and do the shopping on my own. "If you think of anything while I'm out..." I started.

"I know, I'll text you. Georgie and I will be fine. She is going to help me with the stroller again, like this morning. This time, without a deadline, I think we'll be fine."

"Okay." I was nervous about leaving them. He was her guardian, and as difficult as it started off, Sterling's abilities to care for Georgie and know what she needed were improving every day. He didn't need me to hold his hand through the process.

The problem was, I wanted to hold his hand. I liked it far too much when he held mine. I lacked professional distance from the situation. Greta had warned me not to fall in love with the children. She hadn't mentioned anything about the guardian. That went without saying.

I couldn't help myself. Sterling was charming, and kind, and seeing him with Georgie twisted up my insides. I looked at the picture on my phone. Georgie looked like she was his child. Why wouldn't she? And in our coordinating outfits, we looked like a family.

My heart hurt. It was a family I would do anything to be a part of. It was a family I shouldn't be thinking about and should be distancing myself from. But it was the closest to being in a family I had felt in forever, and I liked that feeling. I should have said something about wearing yellow like Georgie the second I walked out that elevator. I should have told Sterling to put a different shirt on. Should have, would have, could have. But I didn't, and now I had a little family photo that shouldn't exist.

Afternoon traffic getting to the store was a mess. But I took my time. I needed to think. What was I going to do? I was falling in love with Sterling. He was a client, and off limits.

15

STERLING

"You came back," I said as Cecelia strolled into the kitchen carrying several plastic shopping bags.

"I wasn't going to take all of this home when Georgie needs it here." She sounded wiped out.

"Two for dinner?" Wayne asked as Cecelia put her bags on the table.

I glanced up at her and raised my eyebrows in question. "Well? You don't have plans for dinner tonight, do you?"

She blinked a few times. "Oh, two, you mean me?" She stared at Georgie, who was in the process of shoving fists full of chopped up chicken and rice into her mouth. The kid was eating everything. Tonight, the mess was minimal.

"Georgie is already having her dinner. Yes, you. Please, have dinner with us."

She smiled, and the simple curve of her lips changed the mood of the entire room. It was as if sunlight broke through storm clouds, bringing warmth and golden light. I felt it in my chest.

"Yes, two for dinner," I answered Wayne. "Show me what you got."

"Let me get the list from the living room," she said.

Georgie cooed, and I made faces at the baby.

"You're starting to actually like her, aren't you?" Cecelia asked as she stepped back into the kitchen, the notepad with her copious notes in tow.

"I... it wasn't that I didn't like her. I didn't know how—"

Cecelia snorted. She made the funniest noises, and it all added to her charm.

"What?" I demanded.

"I bet you aren't used to saying things like 'I don't know,' and 'help me.' Are you?"

"I'm not," I admitted with a huff.

"I can tell. The words sound foreign coming out of your throat."

"Are you teasing me?" I liked it. I liked that she wasn't afraid to talk to me or tell me I was wrong.

"It's only what you deserve for making me blush," she said with a fierce determination.

"Note to self," I said out loud as I scooped up a baby spoon full of rice and faced Georgie. "I need to make Cecelia blush more, don't you think?" I ticked the baby's foot before feeding her.

"Where is the diaper bag, back in her room?" Cecelia asked.

"Here." I stood. "Why don't you feed Georgie and I'll go grab the bag? What else should I get?"

"Anything that needs to go into the bag—diapers, a pack of wipes, clothes."

"Right." I stood there and watched Cecelia smile at Georgie and coo words of encouragement as she fed the baby. It felt hauntingly familiar, like something I had missing from inside me.

I took my time gathering the items I thought would be needed. Instead of grabbing the portrait-ready ruffle dresses I mistakenly thought little girls actually wore on a daily basis—because the only time I saw baby girls, that's how they were dressed—I picked up soft cotton outfits. Three of them. It seemed like overkill, but having already been grossly underprepared once, I'd rather be overprepared going forward.

I shoved everything into the bag and still had my arms full when I went back to the kitchen.

"Oh, wow, okay. Wayne, do you have any gallon-sized zipper baggies?" Cecelia asked. "Oh, and some paper towels."

She started to clean up the highchair and Georgie as soon as she had the towels. She carried the baby's dishes to the sink, leaving the kid in the chair while I spread the contents of the bag over the table.

Georgie sat and cooed and made her baby garbling sounds as I had a lesson in what should go into a diaper bag. Every pocket was filled. It was heavier than before.

"Are you sure this is right?"

Cecelia shrugged. "No. It's righter than what we started today with. The next time you take Georgie out, you'll learn whether it has what you need or not. It's not a static set of must-haves. As she grows, you might need more clothes, or less, or... The point is, you learn and modify as you go."

"Won't you be there to help?" I asked.

"At some point, you'll be on your own. As it is, I'm not here all the time, anyway," she said.

"It's better when you're with us," I admitted.

She pressed her lips together and looked like she was trying not to smile as she blushed.

"Shall I prepare the formal dining room, or would you prefer I clear the table so you can dine in here?" Wayne asked.

I glanced at my watch. It was almost time for him to leave for the evening. I looked at the piles on the kitchen table. No, we were still working on all of this.

"Dining room, please," I said.

He nodded and went back to his work.

"That's so weird," Cecelia said.

"Hmm?"

"Having a butler, it's… not something I think I could get used to," she said.

"Trust me, it is very easy to get used to having someone help out. I grew up with staff, and for a while, I did it all on my own, but at some point, I kept forgetting that laundry didn't do itself, and if I wanted a protein boost after my workout, I had to have the protein powder and peanut butter available to make the shakes with."

"Maybe I could imagine having a personal assistant like that. I hate having to make sure I have enough money loaded into the app for the laundry at the apartment complex. Or I need quarters and a block of time to hang out at the laundromat, just to have clean clothes. And I have to do my own grocery shopping."

"And you have to make sure that I've done all of that for Georgie."

"Yeah, but that's my job. I want to help out. It doesn't mean I couldn't use some help myself from time to time." She lifted Georgie from the highchair, and food cascaded to the floor. Cecelia brushed her off and held her on her knee. "You are a mess."

Georgie yawned and rubbed her little fist into her eyes.

"Bedtime," I announced. "I'll take her."

"Your dinner will be ready by the time you're out of the shower. It will be in the oven," Wayne said.

"Thank you. I'll see you tomorrow."

Cecelia stared up at me, her brow twisted in confusion. "It's her bedtime, but you're taking a shower?"

I cocked my head for her to follow.

"She's a mess, and she needs a bath. I've discovered it's easier to just get in the shower with her. I'm going to get wet, anyway."

"Do you have any laundry baskets?" Cecelia asked.

I shrugged. "I have no idea. I'm not doing laundry."

"No, you're washing a baby. Don't get in the shower. Start the tub. I want to show you something."

I had my shoes kicked off and my shirt off by the time she stepped into my bathroom. She held a white plastic laundry basket, and her expression was one of shock. There was no tub, only a large walk-in.

"I guess the trick I was going to show you isn't going to work."

"What's the basket for?"

"I learned this great trick. You put the baby in a small laundry basket in the tub, so it's a baby-sized tub in the bigger tub. But no tub."

I took the basket and tossed it in the shower on the floor. "It will still help. She can sit in there while I hose her down. I'll show you." I stood and dropped my jeans.

"Mr. Alexander!" Cecelia shouted and spun around, giving me her back.

"I have shorts on," I said with a chuckle.

Georgie and I stepped into the shower. I put her in the basket and turned the water on. I had previously programmed the spray for a lukewarm temperature. It was warm enough so the shower didn't feel cold, but it wasn't hot enough to burn the baby.

I knelt down and washed the baby as water showered down on us.

"This really helps. I don't have to hold a wet, squirmy baby."

"Do you really shower with her like this?"

"This, and she's had a few baths in the kitchen sink. I don't know how, but she's always sticky. The shower makes less of a mess than the sink."

"Make yourself useful. Grab a towel." I turned off the water before picking up the baby.

Cecelia had the towel over her shoulder and wrapped it around Georgie as she took her from me.

"Thanks, I'll be right out."

Cecelia didn't get the hint. She continued to dry off the baby and talk to her with cooing sounds.

"Unless you want to see me naked, you should take the baby to her room. I need to dry off."

She blushed and scampered from the bathroom, slamming the door behind her. She was delightful.

I peeled off the wet shorts and wrapped a towel over my hips. I donned a robe before I crossed the hall and went into Georgie's room.

The lights were already off, with only a soft glow from the cat-shaped nightlight. Cecelia gently rocked Georgie in her arms, humming a lullaby I didn't recognize.

I stepped in close and wrapped my arms around Cecelia with her back to my chest. I watched Georgie yawn and settle into sleep over

Cecelia's shoulder. This felt right, having both of them in my arms at once.

I kept my arms around Cecelia's hips as she lowered the baby into the crib. I rubbed my cheek against hers as she straightened. She turned in my arms, and I captured her lips.

16

CECELIA

With Sterling's lips against mine, my brain just stopped. Everything I had thought about, my resolve to maintain professional, it all evaporated as he pressed against me.

As if of its own accord, my hand slipped between us, and I tugged on the tie that held his robe closed.

He growled low in his throat, and the robe fell open, and I was crushed against his bare chest.

His lips left my mouth, and he placed kisses across my face and along my jaw. I tilted my head to the side, hoping his lips would trail down my neck. I opened my eyes and saw the sleeping baby.

I pressed my palms against his shoulders. "Not in here. This is her space."

"Then come to my space." His voice was low and thick with lust as he slid his hand into mine.

I didn't say anything as he led me back across the hall. He closed the door behind him and let the robe slide from his shoulders. His towel was low-slung around his hips. It was hard to breathe as I admired his body. He was beautiful, a sculpture. And damn if he didn't have six-pack abs.

There was a brief moment, a flicker of warning, where I could stop him. But I didn't want to. He wanted me, and that was as arousing as being attracted to him was. I reached out for the towel as I stepped back to him.

"Can I?" I asked seconds before I yanked, and the towel met the robe on the floor.

I didn't get to admire him for very long. As the towel fell, Sterling made that growling sound again and drew me against him. His lips were brutal as he claimed mine again. I kissed him back with as much ferocity. It was a fight between lips and tongues as we competed to consume each other.

Sterling lifted my yellow tunic over my head and immediately unfastened my bra, discarding it to the side. Cupping both breasts with his hands, he lifted my breasts to his mouth. He sucked an aching nipple into his hot, wet mouth as I clutched him to me. I arched into his touch. A moan escaped my mouth.

My knees went weak. I buckled, but I guess Sterling expected it, or his reflexes were fast. As I went down, he scooped me up and carried me to the bed. At first, I was flummoxed that he could lift me, but of course he could. He was roped and thick with muscles. And he was letting me touch him.

I sank into the mattress as he placed me down and then crawled in over me. I ran my leg over his, reveling in the feel of his damp skin against mine.

His hands skimmed over all of my exposed skin before grabbing my breasts again. He looked deep into my eyes with an intense stare. I could tell he wanted me to know what he was thinking, or maybe he wanted to know what I was thinking. The feeling was overwhelming, whatever it was.

"Yes, I want you. Please," I said. I needed him touching me.

His lips kissed and sucked down my middle until he reached the tops of my shorts. He pulled back and focused as he unfastened the button and zipper. He pulled the shorts and my panties off all at once. He tossed them out into the void that was the rest of his bedroom.

Out there, I knew there was furniture and light, but all I could see, all I cared about was him and the way he touched me.

Sterling lowered himself and placed more kisses along my midsection, continuing down.

I gasped as his mouth found the apex of my legs. My initial reaction was to close my legs, but when his tongue flicked over my seam and tipped between the folds of my pussy, barely licking my clit, I sighed and let my knees fall open. My nerves were on fire, and his tongue was a cool respite. It was both soothing and driving me crazy. He licked and sucked, and the sensations were like lightning in my skin.

I rocked my hips against him, digging my fingers into his thick hair. I wanted to touch him, to hold him, to press him in tighter.

All I knew, all I wanted at that moment was more of his touch, more of him sucking on me. "More, more," I whimpered, desperate with urgency.

"Cecelia." My name was a rumble and a roar as he climbed up my body and crashed his lips back against mine.

It was as if he couldn't get enough of me. I understood the feeling. I wanted all of him.

I pressed my heels against the bed and pushed my hips up against his. I needed his cock. I wanted to feel him. He eased back until he sat on his knees.

"Damn, you are wet." Grabbing his cock, he drew it back and forth over my hot need.

I whimpered and thrust against him, trying to catch him, trying to get him to slip inside me.

He leaned across my body and knocked stuff around on his bedside table. He returned with a foil packet. Using his teeth, he tore it open. The wrapper joined our clothes out in the void. His cock strained as he rolled the condom on.

"Sterling, I need you. I need you inside me," I pleaded.

He fell forward and reclaimed a nipple into his mouth. He sucked me in and then surged into me. I arched into him, wanting him to take everything, needing him to consume me. My nerves were on fire, and my muscles were quivering with excitement.

Everything in my body wanted to scream and clench and explode. I needed him to dive deep into me and become me. I wanted all of him inside, but I also wanted him to take me inside him. We folded into each other.

He pressed his hips hard against mine and moved his mouth back to mine. We were one writhing, combined set of dancing nerves. Sterling rolled us. I don't know how he did it, but he was on his back. I pressed against his chest until I sat back on his hips. I ground against him. The penetration at this angle was almost too much. I needed more. I rocked my hips, bracing against his chest. He laughed as he curled up and grabbed a breast into his mouth. His fingers dug into my hips, guiding me up and down his shaft.

This time, when I whimpered, it was out of frustration. Everything Sterling did to my body felt beyond amazing. The way he managed to make me feel everything in my core or dance along my skin was exceptional, but it wasn't enough. I could feel the pressure building in my core. It built and grew and pulsed, but it never tipped over, never crashed. Every thrust began to feel like a tease as it danced me close but always backed away before I could fall over that magic edge that beckoned and promised euphoria.

"You got this, baby," Sterling growled. He reached between where our bodies pressed together. His fingers wiggled around until he landed on my clit. I cried out when he flicked it.

He began rubbing tight circles around my clit as he thrust into me. I ground and rubbed against his hand. My inner walls began to suck on his cock.

"Yes, yes, oh, God, don't stop."

"I'm not stopping, baby, not until you're screaming."

His words were like magic. I hit the ledge and soared. Every cell of my being clenched and spasmed as the orgasm took over my body. I braced against Sterling and held on as he continued to work my body.

"You've got to scream for me, Cecelia," he demanded.

I could barely breathe. How was I supposed to scream? How was I supposed to do anything? I had no muscle control. My legs were numb. I could barely hold myself in this position.

Sterling dug his fingers into my thighs and flipped us again. He continued to drive hard into me. It was hard, it was amazing, it was going to consume me. Wave after wave of orgasm bounced through my body. Everything clamped so tightly, and then I screamed out his name.

I slammed my fists against the mattress and gasped for air. I needed more, I needed him. He was relentless, and what he did to my body was unadulterated bliss.

He roared and pounded into me before freezing up. I reached up and ran my fingers through the sweat that trickled down his throat as his own orgasm seized his body. I wanted to laugh with the sheer joy of it.

Sterling sucked in a deep breath and let it out as he rolled to the side. As he fell over, he grabbed me so that I ended up halfway across his chest. He let out a laugh. "Damn, you can scream." He glanced over at his bedside table. I followed his gaze. The little white monitor sat there, but no sound came from it. A slow smile spread across his lips.

"Good soundproofing. She's still asleep."

There were other people in the apartment. Mortification swept over me, and my skin heated.

"You're blushing now?" He stroked a finger down my cheek.

"Wayne had to have heard us," I whispered as if being quiet now negated the screaming I did earlier.

"Shh, he already left. He left while you were putting the baby down. It's just us, so you can scream as much as you'd like."

17

STERLING

I rolled over and let my arm fall across Cecelia's shoulders. Only she wasn't there. The pillow was still warm. I hugged it to myself before opening my eyes and sitting up.

"Did the baby wake you?" I asked. I reached for my watch, discarded at some point during the night's activities. Georgie would be waking up soon. She woke up early. I'd change her and give her a bottle and she'd fall right back to sleep. But if she wasn't fussing… "Why are you out of bed?"

"I have to go home and take a shower before I go to work." She jumped a little as she pulled the front of her shorts together and fastened them. I enjoyed how everything wiggled on her.

"You're only going to be coming back here. Why not stay?"

"I have to check in at the office."

"Check in online."

She snorted. "I wish. The system is still down. You know, I expected this kind of discount and duct-taped together operation from public services, but this is a private agency working for lawyers and people like you. They had some kind of disgruntled employee-assisted natural disaster, and with no backup systems or redundancies in place, I still have to file my reports in triplicate."

She sat on the edge of the bed and pulled her shoes on.

"I have to make a report about yesterday."

I raised my brows and rolled so that I could be next to her. "Are you including this in your report?" I teased.

She went pale and closed her eyes. "If they find out I slept with you, I will be fired so fast. This does not get included in the report. This gets mentioned to no one. I don't even want Wayne knowing about this."

"Trust me, the man is paid very well to be discreet. He will not divulge my secrets, and by extension, yours."

She leaned over and looked into my eyes. I could get lost in her when she did that. I pushed up and claimed her mouth. She tasted of the sweetness that followed a rousing night of sexual acrobatics. And she had been rousing and talented. I wanted her back in my bed.

"I'll see you later after I submit my reports. You have your to-do list for the morning. Get Georgie a doctor's appointment, and I'll see what medical records we have on her back at the office. And maybe see if you can find some father-baby classes."

You didn't call them 'Daddy and me'," I teased.

"I thought only I was allowed to call you 'Daddy'?" She kissed me again.

I grabbed her softness into my arms and rolled her back onto the bed, pressing my hips against her.

"Say that again," I demanded.

"And get into more trouble? I don't think so. We don't have time—"

With cosmic bad timing, Georgie's wake up cry sounded through the monitor.

I groaned and rolled off Cecelia.

"Get the baby. I have to go."

Cecelia escaped while I went to take care of the distraught baby.

This morning, Georgie was clingy. She wouldn't let me put her down without much fussing and tears. She felt warm to the touch. I rummaged through the pile of everything Cecelia purchased that had yet to be put away. I found the thermometer. It was the kind that beeped after being put in the ear.

Her temperature was normal, but she was miserable. I gave her a bottle and held her until she fell asleep.

I didn't want to put her back in her crib. I wanted her with me. She was precious, and she was all that was left of Argene. I crawled back in bed and made a barricade of pillows so she couldn't roll off. I researched on my tablet as she slept next to me.

I made a short list of pediatricians in the area to call once office hours began. After checking my email and not finding any updates from the investigator, I sent one to him. Hadn't Argene left any information about the man?

At some point, I fell back asleep alongside Georgie. I woke up with her fingers up my nose and her open mouth biting my cheek in her version of kisses.

"Good morning, little beauty. You must be feeling better." She wasn't fussy or complaining.

"Ow." I clapped my hand over my cheek where she bit me. She bit me. I ran a finger over her gums and found the sharp edge of a tooth breaking through. No wonder she had been unhappy and fussy. She was teething.

"That's it, no biting." I grabbed her and rolled out of bed. She giggled. It was possibly the single best sound in the world.

I carried her into the kitchen and found some yogurt in the fridge. Wayne wasn't in yet, so we were on our own for a while. Cecelia would be in soon. I wasn't worried. For the first time in over a week, I felt like maybe the kid and I would be okay.

Yogurt was less messy than oatmeal, and I was able to leave Georgie in her highchair while I called through the list of pediatricians' offices.

"No, I don't have her medical records. No, I don't know who her last doctor was. No, I don't know." I felt like a broken record. The information I had on Georgie was minimal at best. I didn't even know if she was born in this country. Knowing the life Argene had been living the last time I had contact with her, the odds were not high.

I called the next name on my list.

"Doctor Branigan's office, how may I direct your call?"

"I'm calling to see if the doctor is accepting new pediatric patients?"

"I can help you with that. When is the baby due?" the chipper woman on the other end of the line asked.

"Excuse me? Due?" I asked.

"Aren't you calling to set up for a new patient?"

"I am, but she's already born," I said.

"Oh, I'm so sorry, I assumed you were a soon to be new father making that first baby appointment." I could hear her grimace.

"Look, normally, that wouldn't be a good start for me, but I have this situation, and well, you're now feeling like you need to make things up to me, aren't you?"

"I am so sorry about that. How can I fix this?" she asked.

"I have temporary custody of my niece. She's ten months old. All I have is her birth date. I don't know her medical history. I don't know what shots she may or may not have had. I don't even know if she was born in the States."

"Is that a consideration?"

"Absolutely. And I don't know the health of my sister during the pregnancy. What I do know is this kid eats. She can sit up. She has minimal language, or the beginnings of language. And as of this morning, she has teeth."

"Sounds like you have yourself a situation."

"I do. And so far, none of the pediatricians I've called are willing to accept her as a new patient. Too many unknowns."

"Well, Dr. Branigan does work with a lot of immigrant children at the free clinic."

"What does that have to do with my situation?" I didn't care about the man's charity work.

"That means she's used to having a lot of unknowns when meeting her patients. So, not having any information won't be a hindrance. We can schedule a well baby checkup early next week, if you'd like?"

I did like, and I chided myself for assuming the doctor was a man. I could check getting Georgie a doctor off my to-do list.

The elevator pinged. Even though there was no intercom call from the concierge letting me know Cecelia had arrived, I grabbed Georgie and went to greet her. I felt like showing off that Georgie had an appointment already set up. I was like a little kid eager for praise.

"Mr. Sterling, Miss Georgie, good morning," Wayne said as the elevator doors slid open and displayed that he had arrived, and not Cecelia.

I checked my watch. It was getting late. Georgie would be going down for her first nap of the day soon.

"Did you have an acceptable evening?" Wayne asked.

"Yes, thank you. Dinner was perfect." It was a little dried out, but that had been my fault. I had kept Cecelia in bed for a couple of hours before either of us had remembered we had dinner warming in the oven.

"I expect Cecelia for lunch," I let him know.

"Very good," he responded.

It wasn't very good. Cecelia hadn't shown up before lunch, or even later. I waited for her but gave up and ate when I fed Georgie. I grabbed my phone and checked my messages. Nothing.

I was about to finally call her and see what was taking so long when the phone rang. Caller ID was hers.

"Cecelia, I thought you would be here already. Is everything all right?"

"Is this Mr. Sterling Alexander?"

"It is. Where's Cecelia? Is she okay?" Nerves clenched in my gut.

"I don't honestly know. I was told to call you—"

"This is her number. You're calling from her phone," I growled.

"No, sir, this is the agency's number. I was told to give you a call and apologize. You were expecting a meeting from your caseworker today. We've reassigned your case. Your new case worker will be by tomorrow."

"What happened to Cecelia?" I demanded.

"She has been reassigned to something more suitable to her experience. That's all I can tell you. We do apologize for the inconvenience. Have a good rest of your afternoon."

How was I supposed to have a good afternoon? Cecelia wasn't here, and apparently, I didn't even have her phone number.

18

CECELIA

I couldn't seem to move. I stood perfectly still and tried to make sense of the words Greta was essentially flinging at me. She didn't talk to me. She spoke in my direction. And this morning, she was hurling words at rapid speed.

I should have tried to weave and duck. Maybe some of her barrage would have missed me.

Greta stopped speaking. After I didn't immediately reply, she finally glanced up from her work, her face pinched. "Well?"

"I… I'm confused."

"Cecelia, haven't you been listening?" she snapped.

"Yes, I have been. And I listen every time you tell me anything. When I asked you about the situation with Sterling Alexander, you told me that I was only going to have one client at a time. So, how is it that I'm being punished for doing my job?"

"You're supposed to help locate resources and work through difficult situations your client comes to you with."

I nodded. Yes, that was my understanding, and that's what yesterday's very long day, evening activities notwithstanding, was all about. I opened my mouth to defend myself and say just that when Greta continued.

"It has come to my attention that you spent the day at the zoo with your client."

I cast my eyes around the piles in her office. How had she learned that so fast? I had only mentioned it briefly to Peggy, the other agent in the office pool, when I came in this morning.

"Did you get a sunburn?" Peggy asked.

I had just arrived at my desk and started putting my bags away when Peggy started bombarding me with questions.

"You didn't come in yesterday. What were you doing?" The inquiry continued.

"Yes, I spent a good part of the day outside. I took my client to the zoo, sort of a test run of his ability to take Georgie out into the world."

"How exactly does that work? Did you actually learn anything?" Peggy continued with more questions.

"It was remarkably successful. And when we sat down to review where the problems were, we ended up making a huge game plan, finding all kinds of holes and things that had been missed. Hey, do you know if there are master files somewhere?"

Peggy lifted her brows.

"I have the client file, but there seems to be some information missing. I figure if those records are available, they would be in a master file," I said.

She shrugged. "I've never not had the information I needed. You can check with Greta."

"Thanks. I will."

And then I went back to putting my things away. I went into the break room and poured a cup of coffee. While I was there, I made the necessary copies I needed to fill in to create the report I needed to put together this morning. I returned to my desk. Peggy wasn't at hers, but I didn't put any serious thought to it. We had work to do. I assumed she was doing hers.

I had just started to compose my report when Greta had used the phone intercom system to ask me into her office. She didn't look up as I stepped into her office before she started hurling words at me. At first, I thought she was barraging me with questions because she always seemed to be multitasking and in a hurry. But she never paused long enough for me to respond.

"We are concerned you are falling in love with your client."

Those words were a complete sucker punch to the solar plexus. I struggled for air. There was no way she could have known about my feelings for Sterling. None. And unless they had spies watching me, there wasn't any reason for them to think I had… Nope, I wasn't even going to let that thought enter my mind in case I somehow blurted out the truth of what happened between me and Sterling.

"You are spending excessive time with the baby, taking her to the zoo, watching her in the evening so her guardian can attend events—"

"That's not what happened. I clearly put in my report that the client overstepped and that I—"

Greta waved my concern away. "Regardless, you're being reassigned. We have already made the decision."

What 'we'? The greater office was like a ghost town. I had only ever met Peggy and another caseworker, Jeanne. And as far as management was concerned, I hadn't met anyone. There was one woman who would have whispered conversations with Greta from time to time, but I had no idea who she was.

I was beginning to think that maybe this agency wasn't as renowned as I had thought or been led to believe.

Closing my eyes, I took a few seconds to compose myself. Yes, I did find Georgie adorable, and yes, I was probably too invested in making certain Sterling properly took care of her. I wanted their situation to be a success story. I didn't want Georgie to grow up the way I had—tolerated. And yes, maybe I wanted to be around them more than what could be considered professional interest.

Opening my eyes, I tried to pin my stare on Greta, but she was back at flipping through file folders and muttering how this would be so much easier if someone would just requisition a laptop for her.

I let out a long, slow breath. "Okay. Whom should I return the Alexander file to?"

Greta patted one of the many piles on her desk. "You can just leave it here."

"Is there a master file on the baby? Her guardian"—I didn't know if I could say their names without getting upset— "needs some medical records so he can take her to a well baby appointment."

"Is the baby sick?" Greta asked.

"Not at all. But we agreed yesterday that she should probably have a checkup to make sure there aren't any health issues he should be aware of." I hesitated. She was ignoring me already. "I'll just put it in my report."

"You do that. We'll need a thorough assessment, including all actions taken and where you were in the greater scheme of things."

I nodded. I understood. They needed me to do a complete dump of everything, and not just a bi-weekly progress report. Instead of putting down that on an excursion intended to assess the readiness of the client, we found out how woefully unprepared he is in all phases of caring for a child, and the resulting task list was created, I was going to have to document everything. And I was pretty sure they wanted everything.

Fine. I would write the Georgie and Sterling story thus far for them, leaving out anything that had to do with my feelings on the matter. They were going to get an amazing report from me.

As I started to leave, Greta stopped me. "Cecelia."

"Yeah?" I stopped and waited.

"You need to complete that report and get the file back to my desk by noon. I've got a meeting and will need that so I can reassign the case."

That's not what I hoped to hear. I had wanted her to tell me to take my time.

"You don't have the client's information on your phone, do you?" Greta asked.

"Yeah, so I can call. I did some shopping for them last night."

She shook her head and held her hand out. "That's exactly the kind of thing I warned you about. Getting too close. Unlock your phone, please." She wiggled her fingers until I placed my phone in her hand.

My heart lodged in my throat as she began navigating the screen on my phone. Oh, God, what if she saw the pictures of us at the zoo? We were all in yellow, all looking like a family. My stomach dropped, and panic sweat beaded along my spine.

With deft swipes and pokes, she deleted Sterling Alexander from my contacts. "Does he have your number?" She handed the phone back.

I shook my head, still not sure if I could breathe properly enough to answer. I didn't know if he had it. I couldn't remember. He knew where I lived. He had given me his number in case I needed it while out, but I hadn't called or texted him. "I don't think so."

"Don't go copying out of the file. That's a breach of confidentiality. And a very serious violation, as far as we are concerned. You under-stand what I'm saying?" She looked up at me again, her eyes narrowed.

Why couldn't she just say the words and not expect me to fill in the unspoken blank? "My job is on the line if I use my access to their personal information to contact them now that I'm no longer their case worker."

"Dr. Gareth was right, you are a smart young woman who catches on quickly. Report and file by noon." She patted the pile again.

I had been dismissed.

Greta had taken office gossip and extrapolated that I was getting too close to the client. How often did that happen in this job? Was I simply following in a well-worn path of first-time social workers getting too involved because we wanted to care, and so we cared too much?

I was numb when I sat at my desk. I flipped open the file. Sterling's number was right there. I tried to memorize it, but I knew by the time I was done with my report— more a catalog of events, actions, and subsequent tasks for the client to complete— I would have forgotten the string of numbers.

19

STERLING

This morning, I thought getting dressed for the day before the new case worker arrived would be a good idea. I'm not sure when or why, but I had stopped bothering getting dressed for the day until after Georgie had her breakfast. Maybe it was because, for her, at least, skin was easier to wash than clothes. If she got messy and sticky, a quick rinse in the shower was easy enough.

And for me, I didn't want to repeat the effort. So, I took none. I also think I managed to earn some sympathy points with Cecelia if she showed up and I was still in lounge wear. I looked like the hard put upon, struggling bachelor that I was, thrust unceremoniously into fatherhood.

Surprise, it's not your kid, but here you go, you now have a baby. Make it work. Cecelia was supposed to be the one helping me make it work. Instead, I now had to face down the stern woman who replaced her.

Cecelia may have made me nuts, but she was delightful and fun. This woman had the warmth of a container ship. Yeah, the whole ship.

Wayne showed her into the kitchen upon her arrival. Her name was Peggy Stanholt, and she was nothing if not prompt.

"You're not ready for me?" she asked with an imperious tone.

"Breakfast is taking a bit longer than usual. Georgie is having some difficulties this morning."

This morning was a prime example as to why breakfast was best served while the baby was in just a diaper. After it was clear she would prefer to wear her yogurt instead of eating it, I switched her to oatmeal in case this was her way of letting me know she didn't want yogurt.

She took handfuls of the warm mush and then began yanking on her clothes. Oatmeal was ground into her collar and down her dress front, both inside and out. There was oatmeal in her hair. I was only aware of the oatmeal that I spooned directly into her mouth making it inside. And half of that, she pushed out with her tongue.

She wasn't upset. At least there was that. No, Georgie thought this was great fun. She kicked and giggled and used her baby talk words, whatever they meant.

I had oatmeal smeared down one of my thighs, and my shirt looked like a Jackson Pollock painting if he had created using oatmeal and strawberry yogurt. The pants were Dolce & Gabbana linen. I knew nothing about food stains on designer clothes. I just hoped they weren't ruined.

"You should have had her fed and been ready with your questions by now," Peggy repeated her complaint.

"I understand. However, as you are well aware, dealing with any of this is new for me. I'm learning that Georgie does not function on a timetable."

She harrumphed.

"Wayne," I started. "Why don't you show Peggy—"

"Ms. Stanholt," she corrected.

"Ms. Stanholt to the living room," I continued. "I am aware you are a busy woman, Ms. Stanholt, and that you have other appointments today. However, I simply cannot leave the baby in this condition while you review the status of our case. I will make this quick."

"Why can't he do it?" She pointed at Wayne.

"No, ma'am. I do not provide childcare. This way, please." I shouldn't have gotten so much pleasure as Wayne shut her down. He would hold Georgie long enough for me to take a short bathroom break, but he did not do much more with her. Nor should he. It wasn't his job.

I grabbed Georgie, who giggled as if this were great fun.

"You are a complete mess." I accepted that any mess on her was going to get on me and didn't even try to keep her stickiness off my clothes.

It was easier to hose her off in the shower. I left our clothes in a pile on the shower floor. I pulled on a more casual pair of loose jeans and another button-down before getting Georgie into another cotton dress. Barefoot, but not wanting to keep Ms. Stanholt waiting, I padded across the penthouse to the kitchen, grabbed a bottle already made for the day for Georgie, and carried her into the living room with me.

"Everybody is less sticky this way," I announced as I sat. I held Georgie tucked up against me. She cuddled in and drank her bottle. I think this morning had been entirely too stimulating for her and she was ready to settle down for a bit.

"I see in your file that you were to establish an emergency plan. How is that coming along?"

I shrugged. "Fine, I guess. There is a list on my refrigerator—much to Wayne's dismay—listing the two closest ERs, and emergency phone numbers."

"Why don't I have a copy?"

"Because that was something I pulled together after my last meeting with Cecelia, per her instructions." I leaned forward, hindered slightly by the baby tucked into my side. "Where is Cecelia?"

"Miss Harrison has been reassigned to a client better suited to her skill set."

"She was doing a perfectly fine job with us. Georgie liked her." My gut clenched. I wanted her back. "I found her to be more than competent and acceptable."

The stern woman harrumphed again.

"Have you taken"—she flipped through the folder— "Georgie to the pediatrician yet?" Really? She hadn't bothered to learn Georgie's name?

I shook my head. "No, I haven't."

"She's been to the zoo, but not the doctor?"

"Do you eat sushi, Ms. Stanholt?" I asked.

"I don't see how this is relevant." She rolled her eyes at me.

I stared her down and raised my eyebrows while I waited for her to answer.

"No, I do not eat raw fish."

"Have you been to France? Paris?" I asked.

"Yes, but how is that relevant?"

"You've been to Paris, France, but you don't eat sushi?"

She was fully confused. "Yes, but what does that have to do with anything?"

"That's exactly what you sound like when you ask if she's been to the zoo before the doctor. A is not relevant to B. What would have been nice is your noticing that she hasn't been to the doctor since I gained custody. And instead of trying to shame me for taking her to see some flamingoes and tigers, you should have handed me any medical records you may have for her."

Peggy Stanholt pinched her face and squirmed with indignation. Had she huffed out a, 'well, I never,' I would not have been shocked.

"Georgie has an appointment next week," I continued. "It would have been nice to have been able to provide something more than her date of birth. I should probably get a copy of her birth certificate. I don't even know where she was born."

Ms. Stanholt flashed me a look of concern. "Is that an issue?"

I was already tired of fighting this woman, and we hadn't been talking for very long. This wasn't some meeting to make sure I had what I needed. This was a tug of war. I wanted Cecelia back.

"Ms. Stanholt, I understand that I am seen as a temporary guardian while the lawyers of my late sister's estate exhaust themselves finding Georgie's father based on some cryptic piece of information my sister left. I have come to accept that Argene possibly did that so that after her death, I wouldn't find out that she had no idea who Georgie's father actually was. My sister kept secrets from the family and from me. I sense this might be her last one. My understanding is that while a 'father' was mentioned, his name was not. Knowing what I thought I did of Argene, it's not unreasonable to ask the location of the baby's place of birth."

"As a temporary guardian, I don't see how that is a concern."

It was my turn to huff. "Because I doubt this is a temporary situation. I would like to get my own lawyers lined up to establish full custody when the time comes. Even if Georgie remains my ward, she'll need passports, a Social Security number, and identification. I need a birth certificate to get that taken care of."

"I'll add your concerns to my notes. I see other progress has been made regarding furnishings." She tried to change the subject. "At least you seem to be efficient at bathing the child."

With Cecelia, Georgie and I had been people with needs and she was there to help. Even if she had to scold me about it first. With this woman, we were nothing but boxes to be checked off a list.

"Do you have any information regarding the status of her father?" I asked.

"What do you mean?"

I meant did they have a clue what they were doing? Were they close, or was there really no way of knowing who the man was? George dropped the bottle, and I realized she was sound asleep. I shifted to hold her so she would be more comfortable. It had taken weeks, but holding her was natural. I didn't have to think about it. I realized I didn't want some nameless man who'd contributed some random genetic material to take her away from me.

I needed my appointment with Peggy Stanholt to wrap up soon. I had things to do, the first being contacting my lawyers about establishing a more permanent custody arrangement, and second being contacting the PI I had looking for Georgie's father.

20

CECELIA

I smoothed down the front of my clothes and confirmed I didn't have any crumbs or anything on my shirt. Making a quick mental inventory, I confirmed I had the new client's file with me, a pad of paper, several pens, and a file folder full of resource pamphlets of services I would be recommending.

I stood on the front stoop, inhaled through my nose, and let the breath out on a long, slow exhale before I rang the doorbell.

The door opened immediately. I felt a tickle in my gut and brain. They had probably been waiting for me and watched as I mentally prepared myself. Next time, I needed to remember to do all of that breathing and inventory check in the car, not at the front door.

"Are you the woman from the agency?" a middle-aged man asked.

"Is that Miss Harrison?" another voice called from somewhere inside the home.

"Uh, yes to both," I said with a nervous smile. Showing up at random people's homes before I even knew who anybody was made me nervous. When I had arrived at Sterling's apartment, my nerves had made me cranky and a little bit rude. I didn't want to do that again.

I wasn't here to boss this family around. They needed help.

"Come on in." The man took a step back and welcomed me into their home.

It was a small, cozy home. These were people who worked for a living. They were not heirs to a rich family or CEOs of corporations.

"Thank you so much for coming." A weary looking woman came up to me and took my hand, shaking it. It felt more like she was clutching me for support than welcoming me into their home. "I'm Lucille, and this is my husband, Oscar."

I nodded and smiled. I hesitated because it didn't seem right to say 'pleasure' when it came to meeting them. After all, the circumstances were tragic. "Nice to meet you. You can call me Cecelia. How is your son Hector today?" I wanted to meet him. But if he was having a tiring or difficult day, meeting me could be too much.

"He's asleep right now. If he wakes, would you like to meet him?" Lucille asked.

"I would. But only if he is up to meeting me. I understand he hasn't been home for more than a week. It's all an adjustment, and I wouldn't want to stress him out."

Oscar let out a shaky breath. "Thank you. Ever since he's been home, it feels like everyone wants to come pay him a visit. At the Children's Hospital, he was limited to only family, and only who we said. But we don't have that buffer here anymore. Saying no to visitors who just pop in is exhausting. He only has a couple of good hours a day in him right now."

I nodded. The poor kid. He had been hit by a delivery truck. His neck and back were broken, along with one leg and arm. He suffered many other injuries, but the hardest, the one that he would never recover from, was the damage to his spine that left him partially paralyzed from the neck down and fully paralyzed in his legs.

"I don't want to add to his burden in any way. As a matter of fact, I'm here to make sure you are getting your support needs met."

"The company sent over a rep, and they helped us get the medical equipment. They're paying for everything," Lucille said.

"They don't want us to sue them for millions," Oscar added.

My brows went up, and I looked from one to the other. I shouldn't ask, but my curiosity was piqued. The notes in their case file indicated there was a suit filed by the insurance company, but I didn't see anything about a personal lawsuit.

"We're in mediation," Lucille said. "Money won't give my little boy his legs back, but they were responsible. They need to take care of him."

I nodded as if I understood. I would take note of it for the case file. I had no idea which party had contacted my agency, so I needed to be objectionable.

"Could I take a quick look at Hector's room? I don't want to disturb him, I just want to see what kind of equipment you have in place. I might have some ideas about what else you'll find helpful. And then we can sit down and go over what areas you are having difficulty navigating."

I followed Lucille down a small hall. She opened a door to a room that hummed with equipment. In the middle of a huge medical bed and a wall of motoring equipment was a small child. He couldn't have been more than five or six. Next to him was a stuffed tiger toy. It looked well-loved and worn. My heart clenched and my breath caught in my throat.

Hector was barely seven, and he looked small for his age. Or maybe he simply looked small because of the scale of all the equipment around him. I made note of the oxygen tank and regulators. Meters and monitors. There were plenty of tubes and leads. An electric wheel-chair sat to the side, still in plastic wrapping and with information tags on the handlebars.

I nodded my thanks, and she closed the door. I followed her back down the hall and into her kitchen. She looked years older than I knew her to be when we sat down around the kitchen table. I pulled out the file folder with all of the pamphlets and brochures.

"I think the first thing you are going to have to request is an appropriate passenger van, fully equipped to help you get Hector to and from appointments." I found the van brochure and handed it across the table.

I was there for hours. I didn't bother stopping off at the office to write up my notes. I went straight home. I thought I was going to collapse. I dragged my feet up the steps. It felt like an impossible task. That's what I got for having an apartment on the second floor of a walk-up, no elevators, no choice. Somehow, I managed to get the front door open. I think I closed it before I dropped everything I carried to the floor and staggered to the couch.

Gasping for breath, the tears came, and I started sobbing. I didn't realize I needed to cry. I had felt tired, exhausted beyond reason. Apparently, that meant I needed to let all of my emotions out.

I clutched a throw pillow to my chest and curled in on myself. I gasped for breath and wailed.

I cried because I was so tired I couldn't carry on. I cried for that beautiful child now trapped in his little, broken body. His mind was there, and he was smart, but all of the possibilities of his life had been taken from him. I felt anguish for his family and the struggle they now had. Their bright, joyful son would never be able to run and jump. Eventually, he would learn to play, and his parents would get used to the routine that now made up his life. I cried for the fear and hopelessness I saw in his mother's eyes and the anger I saw in his father's.

I sobbed out all the self-pity I had because I had been reassigned. I didn't understand why Greta couldn't have given me a second assignment if the agency needed to limit the time I spend with Sterling and Georgie? Why did they have to take them away from me?

Because I was growing too attached. And I cried because I had grown very attached, and I missed them. I missed Georgie's wide open-mouthed smile as she learned to control her face. I missed her little grabby hands, and I missed Sterling.

There was no possible way that the agency knew I slept with him. They couldn't. As my feeling of stupidity dragged me back down, I cried even more. I couldn't believe I was such an idiot.

I had slept with Sterling. A client! That was the worst. So dumb, so incredibly dumb. And so incredibly amazing. Part of me knew it had been worth it, just so that I had something to remember when I was old and lonely. A beautiful man had made me feel like I was his every desire.

And of course, that had me crying even more. Of course, Sterling made me feel amazing. He was good. That was experienced and skilled and had nothing to do with anything between us. Because there wasn't anything between us. He was my client.

But he and Georgie didn't feel like clients. They weren't some problem for me to solve. When I was with them, I felt like I belonged. They felt like family.

With a groan, I rolled off the couch. I hit the floor with a jolt. I needed to knock some sense into my head. I cried to the point of swollen eyes, and my sinuses were closed from swelling and snot. I staggered through my small apartment and into the bathroom.

I selected a shower scent bath fizzy, eucalyptus and lavender. It would bubble up and fill the air with a calming smell that should also open my air passages. I turned the shower on, scalding hot, and stripped down.

I couldn't wash away the failures of my day, but the heat felt good to my aching heart and sore muscles. It had been an emotionally long day. All I wanted was to be comfortable and fed. After the shower, I pulled on leggings that felt like a hug and an oversized long-sleeved T-shirt. My hair stayed wrapped up in the towel.

The weather outside was nice, maybe even warm, but I needed the weight and comfort of a blanket. I curled up on the couch and turned the television on. Eventually, I might want something to eat, but for now, I needed something to take my mind away from all the mistakes I had been making. I needed to focus on someone else's problems.

21

STERLING

The woman across from me flipped her hair, again. How many times can a person flip their hair and giggle inanely at nothing in the span of twenty minutes? Too many, far too many.

I was done with this interview. I stood. "Thank you for your time."

"Aren't you going to show me the baby?" she asked.

I shook my head. "I don't think that will be necessary." I swept my arm out, palm up, indicating that she needed to go.

"Mr. Sterling, Ms. Stanholt has arrived," Wayne announced.

"Please show Miss"—fuck, I forgot her name in all the hair flipping. I glanced down at her resume— "Stevens out and Ms. Stanholt in."

Hair-flip Stevens twisted up her lips and sneered at me before flipping her hair, this time in aggravation and with a finality I didn't expect. I had no idea that hair could be so expressive.

"I hope you weren't planning on hiring that woman as a nanny," Ms. Stanholt said with stern disapproval as she stepped into the living room.

"Why is that?" I wasn't planning on having anything to do with her and her hair flipping, but now I almost felt like running after the Stevens girl just to piss this woman off.

"You really should allow me to run a background check on all candidates. After all, my agency is ultimately responsible for the child's wellbeing."

That was a stretch, but Peggy Stanholt had an overinflated sense of responsibility.

"I am happy to submit any candidate for a background check. However, I simply haven't found anyone worth a second interview."

"Have you contacted the agency I recommended?" She asked every question as if she expected me to have completely ignored her recommendations.

I openly and freely admitted that childcare was so foreign and new to me that it wasn't worth playing ego games and struggling my way through it. Not when Georgie was the one who actually suffered.

"Where do you think Miss Stevens came from? Everyone I've interviewed has been sent over from the agency you suggested."

"How many candidates have you already met with?"

I let out a heavy breath. "I met with four yesterday, and I have six lined up for today. And more tomorrow."

The baby monitor carried Georgie's babbling into the living room. "Excuse me, Georgie is awake. I'll be right back. Make yourself comfortable."

I didn't care whether she did or didn't. I jogged down the hall to Georgie's room and opened the door. She stood in her crib, her hands on the railing as she rocked back and forth. She smiled and made more sounds that were almost words. She said something that sounded like *Dada*.

I stopped just before I reached the crib.

She reached out, and this time, she was very clear in her noises. She said, "Dada."

I rushed to her and swung her up into my arms, placing a big kiss on her cheek. "Did you call me Dada?"

She repeated the sound and placed her sloppy open-mouthed, practically a bite, kiss on the side of my chin.

I swung her around and onto the changing table. "You are in a good mood, baby girl."

She smiled and kicked. After she was changed, I picked her up and carried her back out to where Ms. Stanholt waited for us in the living room. It should have been Cecelia. She would have been so excited to hear that Georgie called me Dada. I wanted to tell her, and I hated that I couldn't.

"I have another nanny interview in a few minutes. Are you planning on sticking around?" I asked.

"I thought we had discussed my being available and sitting in for your interviews this morning. Don't you recall?" She sneered down her nose at me.

"It must have escaped my mind," I admitted. I probably forgot about it within moments of her insisting that she be here.

"How many have you already interviewed?"

"Two yesterday, and two so far this morning. I haven't been impressed with any of them yet. Neither has Georgie."

"The baby doesn't exactly have a say," Ms. Stanholt pointed out.

"Maybe not, but I'd rather not expose my ward to someone who scares her."

Peggy Stanholt rolled her eyes.

"Mr. Sterling, your next appointment has arrived," Wayne announced.

"Send her in."

A moment later, a nondescript middle-aged woman followed Wayne into the living room. She interrupted herself multiple times to make baby noises at Georgie, but the baby ignored her and tried to hide in my shoulder.

"She's such a playful little girl," the woman said.

"She can be," I said. But at that moment, Georgie was trying to get the woman to stop looking at her. "She is not at the moment."

"Nonsense. Let me take her." She held out her hands as if she was going to grab Georgie off my lap.

Georgie started to cry as the woman got closer.

I twisted away in my seat. "Not right now." I couldn't read her expression, but she looked disappointed as she sat back down.

"Did you have any additional questions, Ms. Stanholt?" I asked. I was done with the interview.

Ms. Stanholt started to ask something as I took Georgie and left the room. I carried her into the kitchen to get her a bottle.

I set her on the floor next to me as I opened the refrigerator. Georgie grabbed onto my pants leg and pulled up onto her feet.

"Did you just stand up?"

She looked up at me, and her butt wobbled back and forth before she landed on it. I grabbed a bottle and swooped her back up. "You are getting so big and strong."

I was so proud of her. I pressed a kiss to her cheek and hugged her. She took the bottle and leaned back. I shifted her so she could lean back and drink. Her big eyes locked with mine.

"I'm going to tell you something," I whispered so that only she could hear me. "I hope they never find your biological father. You look so much like your mother. I miss her. But I have missed her for far longer than she's been dead. I lost her long ago. I don't want to lose you."

I leaned over and kissed the top of her precious little head.

When I returned to the living room, Ms. Stanholt was alone. The other woman had already left.

"She seemed like a reasonable candidate."

"No," I said as I sat down.

"Why not?" Ms. Stanholt asked.

"She couldn't even tell when Georgie was trying to not be looked at by her. That wasn't some game of peek-a-boo. Georgie was literally trying to hide and get away. I don't want a nanny who is that oblivious to the body language of the baby." I placed the baby next to me on the couch. She leaned against me, not a care in the world.

"You are running out of time. You should have begun the nanny hiring processes from the very beginning."

"Maybe so," I started. "But if that were really the case, your agency would have been more upfront, don't you think?"

She stared at me blankly.

"Fine," I said. "I will find a nanny, and you will get me an update on exactly how the manhunt for Georgie's biological father goes," I said.

Ms. Stanholt pinched her face and began to huff. "I don't have access to that information."

"I need to know. It would be helpful when I contract a nanny to let them know whether it's a short term or longer term position."

We had a bit of a stare-down. I wanted information, and the Stanholt woman just looked pissed.

"Fine, I'll see what I can do."

"Your next appointment is here," Wayne announced. "Shall I send this one in?"

The next two hours passed with interviewing candidates. The meetings didn't last long. The nannies tried to interact with Georgie, but she wanted nothing to do with any of them. One woman even made her cry.

I wouldn't have said any of the candidates were someone I'd consider calling back.

"Are you planning on coming back to the interviews I have scheduled tomorrow?" I asked as Ms. Stanholt gathered her things.

"I trust you can make initial assessments without my being here. I would like to be included in the second round of interviews."

I nodded. I was going to have to call a second agency at this rate. I picked up Georgie after Ms. Stanholt left. I carried her to the kitchen. It was time for lunch, and then it would be time for her afternoon nap.

It had been a long morning. As Georgie crammed little bits of chicken and rice into her mouth, I popped a full-sized chicken nugget into my mouth. It seemed easier to just ask Wayne to make one meal for the two of us. Just as Georgie was becoming a functional kid, I was becoming the parent of a soon to be toddler. I chuckled as warmth spread over me. I liked the thought of being her father.

But there was an obvious hole in the little family we were becoming. Cecelia was missing. She belonged here with us.

22

CECELIA

Today wasn't nearly as emotionally draining as the day before. I spent my day writing up reports and making phone calls tracking down resources for Hector's parents. Not having to look them in their heartbroken eyes made a difference. A slight difference.

The entire situation was overwhelming, but having some distance, even a modicum of distance, made a difference. It was still emotionally hard, but by the end of my workday, I didn't feel like I was going to dissolve into a puddle of tears.

I stopped for Chinese takeout on my commute home. I felt beat-up and sad. I didn't realize how emotionally difficult this job would be. I parked in my assigned spot and gathered everything together. I really needed to get myself a couple of tote bags. My inability to carry everything was blatantly obvious for once. I had to accept that I only had two arms and two hands. With the bag containing my dinner hooked over my elbow and file folders precariously balanced in my grasp, I turned the corner and started climbing the stairs to my apartment. I needed a free hand for the railing.

I kept my eyes on the stairs in front of me for balance. I didn't look up until I heard a familiar happy baby gurgling sound. I gripped the handrail tightly and looked up. I held my breath the entire time.

At the top of the stairs, in front of my door, stood Sterling. He held Georgie in her car seat. They were waiting for me. I let out my breath on a long exhale.

"Sterling?"

"Cecelia, you're finally home," he said with a chuckle.

"Finally? Yeah, that's how it feels." I started climbing again.

"I'd offer to take some of that for you, but I'm afraid you might drop something." He backed up and let me unlock the door.

Once inside, I crossed to the kitchen and deposited everything in my arms onto the table. My heart was pounding with a fast, hard thudding that shook me to my toes. It was difficult to catch my breath, like I had been running a race. I was scared to turn around.

"Cecelia." Sterling's voice was low and soft against my ear. His hand was hot on my arm as he turned me into his chest.

"Cecelia," he murmured again seconds before his lips were on mine.

I moaned into him. I wanted this, dreamed of this moment when we would be back together. The warmth that spread through my body seized up and crashed back in on itself. I pushed away from him.

"Sterling, no," I whimpered. Stepping back from him was more than emotionally difficult. It was physically painful. "What are you doing here? You can't be here."

He gestured at Georgie, who was cooing and squirming in her car seat. "We missed you."

I rushed over to her and removed her from the car seat. I hugged her to me as she grabbed my face and made soft sounds of recognition. She smelled like clean baby and powder.

"I missed you too, but you really shouldn't be here," I said as I sat on the floor, Georgie in my lap. If I held her, I wouldn't feel the desperate urge to hold Sterling.

Sterling crouched down in front of me. He took Georgie's little hand. "So much has happened in the few days since you've gone." He directed his next words to Georgie, pitching his voice higher. "Haven't they, Georgie? So much."

She cooed and babbled.

"Did she just say Dada?"

Sterling laughed. "She did." His smile was broad and full of pride. "And you should see this."

He scooped Georgie out of my lap, setting her feet on the floor but holding her upright. He shifted his grip from around her ribs so that he was just holding her hands.

She stood on her own. She wobbled a bit, but she was standing up.

"She's standing?"

Sterling shook his head. "She's walking. Not very well. She took her first step a couple of days ago. She only takes one or two at a time, but..."

We both waited to see if she would take a step. Instead, she sat down on her bottom.

Sterling lifted his eyes from gazing on his ward, full of pride, up to mine. "You should have been there. Cecelia. The agency sent over this horrible woman. She's supposed to be helping me find a nanny."

He shook his head.

"You actually helped me. You made sure I knew how to care for Georgie. Now, the priority seems to have shifted. No one cares whether I know how to care for Georgie. No one cares that I want to keep her."

I snapped my head up. "What?"

He was smiling. He held Georgie in his lap. They looked like they belonged together. The family resemblance was strong. If he adopted her, no one would ever doubt she was his daughter.

"Yeah, I've already decided. I'm keeping her."

"But what about her bio-father?" I asked.

Sterling was quiet for a moment. He let out his breath and began adjusting Georgie's clothing. He didn't look up. "My sister, Argene, was a hot mess. I loved her dearly, but... when I learned of her passing and how she died, I wasn't surprised. Saddened. It still makes me sad. She was a magical girl. She was able to reject how we were raised. She was a fairy child, if they were real. She did not want to be bogged down by the appropriate societal expectations my parents raised us with. Argene escaped to see the world. And to party. She chased musical festivals and raves. She followed party DJs across the Mediterranean. It wouldn't surprise me if one of them was Georgie's father. But..." He shrugged.

"I loved Argene, but I seriously doubt she had a clue who Georgie's father really was. Your agency is never going to be able to locate him. And if they do, I am prepared to make it worth his financial while to sign over custody."

"You really are going to fight for Georgie?" I asked.

"I fight when it's important. Georgie is important." His gaze locked with mine.

I felt the intensity of his conviction in my entire body. It was a thrum of energy, intense and magnetic. It pulled me to him. I rolled up onto my knees and leaned into him. It was my turn to kiss him.

He cupped the back of my neck and held me to him as our lips slid together, our tongues danced. The kiss felt full of righteous conviction. This kiss felt like he was telling me he wanted to keep me.

I was breathless when the kiss ended. Sterling still held me to him.

"We can't… I can't. Sterling, you shouldn't even be here," I whispered.

Burning started behind my eyes, and my sinuses stopped up. Damn it, I didn't want to cry. I didn't want him to see how weak I was. I needed to have the same conviction he did. I eased away from him and onto my feet. I wiped at the tears that fell without my permission.

"If they find out you're here, it's my job. I can't lose my job. I think they somehow found out about us, and that's why they moved me."

"How?" His voice was low, almost a growl. "How would they know about us?"

I shrugged and paced in a circle. "I wanted to call you so badly. My boss actually took my phone and erased your number from it. She didn't trust me to do that myself. I went over all the training materials they gave me. And nowhere, nowhere in that information does it say that going to the zoo with you and Georgie was against protocol. It actually said observed outings are encouraged. It said I should make sure you know what you're doing in different scenarios."

"Well, the only scenario they are interested in right now is setting us up with a nanny," Sterling said flatly.

"I mean, a nanny is a good idea. At some point, you are going to have to go back to work, right?"

He nodded. "Yeah, my leave of absence will end, and I will need care for Georgie. But I've got weeks yet for that. But this Peggy Stanholt is pushing the nanny agenda."

I spun around and stared at him. "Peggy? You got Peggy?" I closed my eyes and let out a heavy sigh.

"You know her?"

I nodded. "I'm pretty sure she's the one who tattled on me about the zoo trip. I had done nothing wrong. She must have said something.

Crap." Panic welled up inside. "You need to leave. Sterling, you and Georgie can't be here."

"Cecelia," he started.

"No, Sterling, I don't want to get into trouble. And I don't want to give them any excuse to take Georgie away from you."

"They can't take Georgie," he said calmly and firmly.

I wasn't calm, and I felt wobbly, not firm, in my conviction. I was scared and confused. I didn't want to lose my job, but more importantly, I didn't want Sterling to lose Georgie.

"You don't have custody of her yet. You need to go, and you shouldn't come back. Don't come back."

23

STERLING

I stared at Cecelia in disbelief. "You don't really mean that," I said.

"Yes, I do." She shook like a nervous fawn on unstable legs.

In a single move, I was on my feet and crossed the small space to her. Georgie squealed as I tucked her under my arm like a football. Reaching out for Cecelia, I grabbed her around her back and pulled her against my side. She braced her hands against my chest. I searched her face, looking for the truth in her eyes.

"You're a terrible liar," I said.

She closed her eyes and leaned into me. We stayed like that for a long moment, and then she moved as if she were dancing. She took Georgie and carried her back to the car seat. "I'm going to miss you."

She placed a kiss on the baby's head and began strapping her into the car seat.

Sitting back on her heels, she looked up at me. "I'm going to miss you too. You have to go."

"Do you honestly think you can get rid of me this easily?" I demanded.

She closed her eyes and shook her head. "I don't *want* to get rid of you, Sterling. I *have* to. Don't you understand?"

I held my hand out to her and helped her to her feet. She wouldn't look at me. I tipped her face up to mine with a finger under her chin. Brushing my lips over hers and then kissing her on her brow, I muttered, "I understand, but I don't like it."

She wrapped her arms around herself and turned away as I picked up Georgie's car seat. I looked at her back, longing for her to turn around. "Cecelia."

She only shook her head and would not turn around.

With a heavy breath and a tightening in my chest that felt like loss, I carried Georgie out of the small apartment. Once outside, I pulled out my phone. "Pick us up. We're outside."

The driver wouldn't be far. The car pulled up as we reached the sidewalk. Once the baby's car seat was strapped in, I sat back. Cecelia should have been with us. This felt too much like defeat. And I wasn't going to accept this was the only option we had.

"Step one," I began out loud.

"Sir?" the driver asked.

"Talking to the kid," I said.

"Yes, sir." The intercom clicked off.

"Where were we? Yes, step one, I need to secure your custody. At least to the point where Cecelia doesn't think there is a threat of the agency snatching you away from me. Step two, I really do need to find you a nanny. But I'm not hiring someone from that agency Peggy Stanholt suggested. I don't trust her to not put a spy in our lives. So, where does that leave us?"

Georgie fussed. She was right, we weren't in a strategically good position. Not if the very agency that put Georgie with me was somehow a threat to my keeping her.

I hit the intercom. "Take us to Highland Park Village."

"Very well, Sir."

When we arrived, the driver assembled the stroller as I unbuckled the car seat.

Georgie and I spent the evening shopping. I had an idea of what I needed. I assumed I would find it all at the shopping center. Georgie and I stopped for what was more of a late snack than a dinner. I discovered she seemed to enjoy lobster bisque and a variety of cheeses and breads.

"You've been holding out. I think it's time Wayne started making my old favorites again. You can eat my food. I am not exactly a fan of chicken nuggets." I spoke to Georgie as if she completely understood me.

When our shopping was finished, I called the car to come pick us up. "I need a phone."

"How do you mean, sir? I can take you to your service provider's retail location."

"Yes, that."

By the time we arrived home, I had a gift to package up for Cecelia, and Georgie was fast asleep. Wayne waited for our arrival at the elevator to unload the packages.

"Did you have a successful outing?" he asked.

"Did I get everything done I intended? No. But Georgie and I did not run into any issues, and we even successfully found food. So, that was a success."

"Shall I unpack everything?"

"No, just put it on the table in the kitchen. We can deal with it in the morning. I need to get Georgie into bed."

"Then I will wish you a good evening now, and I will see you in the morning," Wayne said as I carried Georgie down the hall.

She fussed slightly before calming back down. I sat with her for a long while, gently patting her back, soothing her to sleep. How had this tiny little person come in and changed everything in such a short amount of time? I would do anything to protect her. And to think I didn't even know of her existence a few short weeks ago.

Reluctantly, I left her bedside. I tucked the baby monitor into my pocket, but I knew her patterns now. She would sleep for a good, long while.

I began rummaging through the packages, getting everything set up the way I wanted. The longest part of the entire process was wrestling the phone out of the thick plastic shell case. I set the account to my credit card and programmed my number into it.

Wayne kept a corner of the kitchen set up like a home office for himself. I raided his supplies and found paper. Writing the note was easy.

I'm not giving you up. Don't give up on us. My number is programmed. There is no reason anyone at your job needs to know.

I folded it and tucked it in against the phone. I carefully unwrapped the tote bag I purchased and placed the phone in the inner pocket before rewrapping everything meticulously. In the morning, Wayne would arrange for the gift and some flowers to be delivered.

All I had to do now was wait. I was not particularly a patient man, and this was going to chew at my resolve. Eventually, I made my way to bed. Tomorrow was going to feel like a very long day.

In the morning, Georgie woke me. We did our routine, a clean diaper, a warm bottle, snuggle time, and back to sleep for a few hours before beginning the day. Wayne had arrived by the time we were both dressed and ready for the day.

"More nanny candidates today, Mr. Sterling?" Wayne asked.

"Thank you for the reminder. I need to cancel those. Could you arrange to have this delivered along with some flowers to Cecelia? Her address is on a note page under the gift bag. Time it so that it arrives after she has gotten home after work."

He nodded, and I took Georgie with me into my home office. I had calls to make and appointments to cancel. Georgie was a disruptive assistant. She smashed her hands against the keyboard of my laptop and tried to grab my phone out of my hands. If I put her down in her bounce toy, she complained that I was ignoring her. Everything took longer than it needed to. My foul mood was reflected by the baby, and neither of us had a very nice time. We were both cranky and whiny.

The day dragged, and it was an eternity of time before my phone rang with the one call I had been waiting for.

"Cecelia," I said as I answered the phone.

"Sterling, what have you done?" she asked.

"Don't you like the gift?"

She laughed. "Thank you, the tote bag is very thoughtful. But I think it cost more than I spent on my car."

I laughed. "You can't keep carrying everything in your arms."

"What am I going to tell them at work?" she asked.

"I don't understand," I said. She wasn't making sense. "It's a tote bag. You could have bought it yourself."

"No, Sterling, I couldn't have. This bag costs more than I make in two months."

"Does that mean you aren't going to accept it?"

"What?" she practically shrieked. "It's not every day someone just gives you an Hermès bag. Hermès, really? I should tell you I won't accept it, but I do love it. And the phone…"

"There is no way they can trace the phone. If you leave it at home, your work won't even know about it," I explained.

"I know, but why?" she asked.

"Because I want to talk to you, and you won't call me on your own phone even with my phone number in those files you carry around."

"Work," she said.

"Exactly. I gave you the phone, I gave you my number. They can't claim you did anything wrong. I'm the one out of line here."

"You're not out of line." She giggled.

I missed that sound. I missed her.

"I liked the flowers too." Her soft voice reached through the phone and went straight to my groin.

"Are you going to let me see you again?" I asked.

"You know I have to say no."

24

CECELIA

I couldn't believe the tote bag Sterling sent over. It was two-toned leather and gorgeous. There was no way I would be able to haul my stuff to work in it and pass it off as a thrift shop find. I felt like an idiot just petting it, but it was the most luxurious thing I had ever owned.

The phone with his number already programmed, that was a nice touch too.

As much as I professionally knew there needed to be distance between us, my heart pounded with joy at the sound of his voice. After I got off the phone with him, I went to the mall and bought myself a tote bag. The one I ended up with wasn't nearly as nice, and it cost about a thousand times less. But I needed a bag, and Sterling's gift, as outrageously expensive as it was, reminded me that I really needed a bag.

I stroked the side of the fabulous Hermès bag before I left for work, the cell phone that was just for him tucked inside. I had a day of making reports and following up on services that were needed for Hector and his family.

When I got into the office, Peggy was there. My gut clenched. She had betrayed me to get to my client. That's the only explanation I could think of. Why else tell Greta the very things I was going to include in my report?

"Anything interesting happening in your world?" she asked with a sing-song voice.

I shook my head. "No, should there be?"

A sense of guilt washed over me. There was no possible way she could have known that Sterling sent me an expensive gift. She shrugged and rolled her eyes. Her lips pinched in a weird smile, like she was keeping a secret.

"No, nothing is going on. Look, Peggy, am I even allowed to ask you how the baby is doing?"

"What baby?" she asked.

Really? She was pretending to not know who I was talking about, yet she was playing games like she knew some secret. I wasn't about to let her know there was a secret that I wasn't telling her. That was between Sterling and me.

"That's how it's gonna be? Got it," I said. I wasn't in the mood to play her games. "Not my client, not my information."

I sat down and began organizing my files. My new work-specific tote bag was going to make my work life a lot easier.

"That's a nice bag," Peggy said, pausing as she strolled past my desk.

"Thanks." I didn't feel like telling her I got it at the strip mall and that if I had gotten it at the department store, it would have cost me twice as much. And I didn't need to confess I was carrying it because there was no way I was going to carry a five-thousand-dollar Hermès bag that was gifted to me.

I pasted a fake smile on my face and told myself there was no possible way she knew. None whatsoever. If she had those kinds of resources, there was no way she would be stuck in a job like this.

And yes, barely two months into this job, I was feeling stuck. It wasn't the work, it was the bureaucracy and the ridiculous situation of being stuck without computers and making photocopies in triplicate. A situation I had been told more than once would be getting fixed any day now.

When I didn't give Peggy whatever it was she wanted from me, she left in a bit of a huff.

I wrote my reports. I made my calls. I even had a short visit with Lucille. I brought her a delivery of some groceries, and we spent the time reviewing all the different grocery store pick up and delivery options within a ten-mile driving distance. She had more than her hands full with taking care of her son. She didn't need to spend hours at the grocery store when with a few clicks, she could have what she needed delivered.

The first thing I did when I got home was rush into my room to see if the bag was still there. The box sat on my bed where I left it, and inside, the silk bag that held the leather tote. It hadn't been a dream. It was real. I stroked the supple leather. I picked up the phone where I had left it in the box, next to the bag. A single message said, *call me.*

There was a knock on my door just as I was about to press *Call.* I left everything on my bed and crossed the apartment and opened the door.

"Delivery for Miss Harrison."

"That's me," I said. The delivery guy didn't look like mail delivery, and there were no flowers. "I wonder what I ordered. I buy so much stuff online, I forget. That ever happen to you?"

He handed over a zoo gift shop bag. "Not that kind of order. Have a good evening."

I took the bag and closed the door. I carried the new present back to the bedroom and picked up the phone again. It rang three times.

"What did you send me?" I asked as I opened the bag.

"So you got it? Do you like it?" Sterling was laughing on the other end of the call.

I pulled a gorilla figurine out of the bag. It was made from recycled flip-flops in Africa. I had admired it the day of our zoo trip. There was something oddly adorable about it.

"You remembered," I said. "Thank you. You shouldn't have."

"No, I should have. I should have that day."

"Sterling…" I didn't know what to say.

"Are you going to come back to us?" he asked. "And don't say you can't. I miss you. Georgie misses you."

"I miss you too. But…"

"I know, I know, work. They don't have to know. You are allowed to have a private life, aren't you?"

I sighed. It felt like I wasn't allowed to have the private life I wanted.

"Supposedly. But who has time, right?" I tried to joke.

"If we both happen to be at the same place at the same time, your job can't fault you for that, can they?"

"What are you thinking about, Sterling?" I asked.

"Meet us someplace. This weekend. There's a park. No one from your work will run into us there." His voice was soothing and convincing. "Georgie would love to see you. She's walking more. You know you want to see her."

He knew what he was doing. He knew my weakness. I adored that child.

"Fine," I acquiesced. "I'll meet you. We can have a picnic. You're bringing the food."

"You're a demanding woman."

I laughed. I missed his sarcastic wit. "That's part of the job. I have to tell you what to do because you don't know anything."

"I'm not your client anymore, remember?" he teased.

"Unfortunately. Thanks for the reminder." I flopped back on my bed. "I don't know if this is such a good idea."

"You can't back out on me now," Sterling said. "You already agreed. You don't want to break Georgie's little heart."

"She doesn't know," I said.

"Maybe not, but if she did. Everything will be fine, Cecelia."

"What did you do today?" I didn't want to focus on my paranoid concerns that Peggy was somehow following me.

"I found a nanny. At least I think I did. The first person the other agency sent over. And Georgie seems to like her. She'll start part-time as soon as she passes a background check."

"I thought nanny agencies already did all of that, you know, bonding and background checks," I said.

"Yeah." He chuckled. "They do. Ms. Stanholt wants any nanny to have a background check run through you guys."

That didn't make any sense. Why do redundant work? I think I kept Sterling talking just so I could hear his voice. The weekend seemed so far away. It was going to be days before I got a chance to see him. And it was going to be in a park, so I wouldn't get to touch him or kiss him.

"I miss you," I blurted out.

"That's what I keep telling you, Cecelia. I miss you too. It's not the same here without you ordering me around."

I laughed. "You make it sound like I'm the one in charge."

"You are, aren't you? In charge of knowing how to take care of Georgie, in charge of pointing out all the things I don't know."

God, his words were so sexy. "I'm not in charge of anything, least of all you."

"I like it when you tell me what to do."

I felt a blush heat my cheeks. "Sterling, are you flirting with me?"

"Most definitely. You could come over now, you know. We could have dinner, you could play with the baby, help me put her to bed."

That's how he seduced me the first time. "That's how we got into trouble last time." I giggled.

"I wouldn't call that trouble. And if that's trouble, it's worth it. You're worth it." His voice was a rumble that made my toes curl.

25

STERLING

Georgie crawled over the picnic blanket I had spread over the grass. I lounged as she crawled back and forth and then used me to stand up. She tried to walk but ended up landing on her butt after a few steps. Wayne had prepared a basket and a cooler bag with our picnic lunch.

We had food, we had sunshine, and now we needed Cecelia.

"This place is hard to find," Cecelia said as she took long, exaggerated steps to get to us.

She was carrying the bag I had given her and dropped it on the edge of the blanket and sank to her knees. She glanced at the bag. "Maybe I should have brought a different bag. I shouldn't put that in the dirt."

"It's just a tote bag. It's fine," I said.

"It's an expensive tote bag, Sterling. And I love it. Thank you. I'm not used to carrying around things that cost so much money."

"But you are using it," I pointed out.

"I didn't want to be rude. You bought me a thoughtful gift. I wanted you to know it is appreciated and useful. Are you going to walk?" Her attention shifted as Georgie began taking wobbly, tentative steps in Cecelia's direction.

They both giggled, and Cecelia cheered as Georgie reached her.

"This is a nice place. How did you find it?" Cecelia asked. "I had a hard time, and I had a map. This isn't the kind of park you stumble upon."

"I asked around. I wanted something not on the beaten path. This way, your coworkers won't accidentally stumble upon us. Ready for lunch?" I began opening the basket and removing various items, wrapped sandwiches, sliced cheeses, crackers, and fruit already cut into bite-sized pieces.

"Wow, you thought of everything," Cecelia said as she snapped the lid off a glass container. She pulled out a small piece of pink fruit and handed it to Georgie. "We don't have to cut anything down to her size. Oh, except maybe the pickles," she said after opening another container. "Does Georgie even like pickles?"

"Loves them. I discovered she likes food, and not just chicken nuggets and rice. I've been trying her on different things. She seems to love pickles, and I read about giving her a full pickle. She just sort of mauls it. With only the two teeth, she can't really get a good bite, but keep an eye on her if you give her one anyway."

I continued to pull out and loosely arrange the food. Georgie was in grabby hands mode, so it worked out best to not open everything unless we were serving it onto our plates.

"I can't believe you packed real plates," Cecelia said.

"What do you mean?"

She sat across from me, her legs folded in front of her, Georgie perched in the space. Her plate had more of the things that Georgie could feed herself. Cecelia picked out a stuffed olive from its container and popped it in her mouth and chased it with two slices of cheese.

"I mean, dishes and not paper plates. Even all of the containers are the good stuff and not worn-out plastic to-go containers you'll toss before packing up and going home."

"Is that how you picnic?" I asked.

"Are you in the mood for a lecture on the differences in socio-economic activities?" she teased.

I shook my head. "Not really, but shoot."

"When I was a kid, a picnic was a loaf of bread, a jar of peanut butter, and a jar of jelly. We'd take plastic knives and a roll of paper towels. Make sandwiches there, until we were out of bread. And toss every-thing, unless there was a lot of peanut butter and jelly left. If we were being fancy, my dad would buy a bucket of fried chicken and all the sides. We'd eat off paper plates. There wasn't an actual wicker basket, maybe just a plastic grocery bag."

"Are you saying I made this too complicated?"

"You made it?" she asked.

"Okay, fine, are you saying Wayne made this picnic too fancy?"

She nodded. "He made it rich. I've been thinking about something you said. And maybe I wasn't actually doing you any good. I wasn't treating you like someone who has the resources to have picnics like this put together or as someone who drops five grand on a leather tote bag. I was treating you as someone who needed to learn how to take care of a child when in reality, I probably should have spent more time focusing on getting you set up with a nanny."

"Why would you say that? Those first few days with Georgie were incredibly hard and completely worth it. I learned that she is her own person, but she isn't a mini, logical adult. I learned so much about her, about babies, about myself. I wouldn't have gotten any of that if you had swept in and put a nanny in place. Look, Cecelia, I was raised by nannies, not my mother. I was raised with old-fashioned ideals that somehow linked my masculinity to my ability to care for a tiny human. Had my parents gotten their way, I never would have changed a diaper or learned how to heat up a bottle. I thought I was doing great all on my own."

I took a sip of the sparkling water that had been packed instead of champagne.

"Argene, Georgie's mother, ran away so many times because our parents wanted her to fit into this ideal expectation of a young lady in society. Everything was so much stricter for her than it ever had been for me. It wasn't until she was fourteen or fifteen that I even saw her as her own person. She was a troublemaker, so she was sent away to school. She was an embarrassment to the family. I don't recall exactly what my mother said, but that summer, she threatened to not take Argene that summer, said she was too wild. Mother took us to islands. She loved islands. Majorca, Greece, the Caribbean. We would go with her for weeks every summer. My struggling sister was being punished for struggling. We lost my mom the next year, and my father, who had never once gotten to know his only daughter, lashed out at her. I tried to step in. I tried to be an older brother, but it was too little, too late. I'm never going to be able to make that up to her."

"But maybe you can." Cecelia set her plate down and lifted Georgie off her lap before leaning in and putting her hand on my chest. Her voice was low, and her words were soft. "You can make it up to Argene by taking care of Georgie properly, giving Georgie the love of a father that Argene never had."

I covered her hands with mine and closed the gap between us. Her lips were cool and tasted like berries. The urge to deepen the kiss welled up and then was smashed down as Georgie bashed her way between us.

Cecelia sat back with a laugh as I scooped Georgie to me. I closed my eyes and leaned against her precious little head. I had failed Argene. That guilt was mine. But I was not going to fail Georgie.

"Have you heard any news from the investigators trying to locate her biological father?"

I shook my head. "We submitted a DNA test the first week she was in my custody. I swabbed my cheek too, so that we could confirm there was a maternal relation match between us. That's the only relation match that any system has pinged."

"What if her father's family used a different company?"

I nodded. "That's part of the search. As I understand it, they send out Georgie's records with a DNA match request for a paternity search. If anyone on his side has done one of those ancestor heredity searches, hopefully, they'll get a match."

"You're lying," Cecelia said. "You don't want him to be found."

"You're right. Hopefully, there will never be a match. I don't think they are as big in Europe."

"You think her dad is European?"

I shook my head. "I have no idea, and I don't want to speculate. We have at least five more months before absentee parental rights are terminated. Longer, if those lawyers Argene had working for her have the money to chase after this. But their contact information is being withheld."

Cecelia grimaced. "Yeah, confidentiality and protecting the client."

"Shouldn't protecting the client allow me to choose who my case manager is? I want you back. I like having you around, but also for Georgie. You push me to be a better father to her."

A slow smile spread on Cecelia's lips. "I like how you are calling yourself her father."

I let out a heavy breath. "I didn't know I wanted kids. I actually thought I didn't want them until I had her in my life. I can't imagine, and I don't want to imagine, not seeing her grow up. That's not an option. So, you see, I need you, we need you. How else am I supposed to learn how to raise her?"

26

CECELIA

This had to be one of the stupidest things I had ever done. I stared at the elevator door as I rode up to Sterling's penthouse.

"Miss Cecelia," Wayne said as the elevator doors slid open. "Welcome back. Mr. Sterling and Miss Georgie are in the kitchen. Will you be needing a coffee this morning?"

"No, thank you, and I'm not here." It felt wrong saying that. I shouldn't be here. This was a mistake.

"Precisely. Mr. Sterling has filled me in, and discretion is a substantial part of my job," he said with a curt nod.

Now I was curious. What secrets did Wayne know? Probably every woman Sterling ever slept with—not that I wanted to know or was curious. I just couldn't think of any other secrets Sterling could possibly have.

I followed Wayne into the kitchen. Sterling sat in front of Georgie's highchair, spooning oatmeal into her wide-open mouth. She looked like a little bird waiting for mama bird to feed her. He wore a tight gray T-shirt and soft lounge pants. Did he know how sexy that look was? Or how incredibly attractive his being a loving, responsible father to Georgie was?

"I shouldn't be here," I blurted out. My gut twisted into knots.

"Stanholt isn't scheduled to come over, so you wont run into her in the elevator or anything, if that's your concern," Sterling said. He gave me a dazzling smile before returning his attention to feeding Georgie. She was noticeably cleaner than the last time I watched him feed her. He didn't have oatmeal smeared all over himself, either.

"But I do have an appointment, so let's get started. This isn't a social call." I put my work tote bag on the table and pulled out a chair.

"What happened to the bag I gave you?"

"I can't carry that bag around on my salary. Too many questions. Are you ready to go over your lists? Do you have copies for me?"

"Didn't you keep copies?" Sterling asked.

"I had to turn everything in. You're not my client, remember?"

"I haven't forgotten, but you are certainly acting like I am. Bossing me around, telling me what to do," he said. I thought I heard a chuckle in his voice, but I couldn't be sure.

I let out a long, weary sigh and slumped into the chair. "Sorry," I said. "I'm nervous about this whole thing. I shouldn't have come over before work."

"I'm glad you did. Happy to see you. But if coming in before your other appointments is going to be too stressful, how about you come back after work? We can have dinner and I can show off my ability to get Georgie and me through a complete day."

It was nice to see him. And I had missed Georgie, even though it had only been two days since our picnic. "Tonight?"

"Yes, tonight. Do you have your phone with you?"

I shook my head. It was safe and sound and tucked away with the tote bag.

"That doesn't matter, just come."

I nodded my head. "Okay. I will. I should get going. I need to pick up some groceries on my way."

"You do grocery shopping now?" Sterling asked.

"I want to help out. A quick shopping trip is just a drop in the bucket for this family. It's the least I can do, especially since I'm already late." I gathered my things and started to head out.

Sterling caught my arm. I twisted to look at him. He tugged, and I leaned over. His lips pressed to mine. "I'll see you later."

Starting off the day with a kiss from Sterling had me floating. Everything seemed so much easier. Even Lucille and Hector were having a good day. I wasn't scheduled to go into the office at all, so as soon as I left their house, I went home to change.

I knew I didn't have to get dressed up for dinner with Sterling and Georgie. I just didn't want to be in my work clothes. I put on a cute dress and a pair of sandals and headed back out to his apartment.

I waved at the door man. It was the same one as this morning. "I'm headed up to Sterling Alexander's," I said as I continued to the elevator that would take me all the way to the top of the building.

"Just a moment, please," he said.

I stopped and blinked at him a few times. He knew me. He always just waved me up. Holding up a finger indicating I should wait, he picked up the phone. He nodded a few times before putting the receiver down. "Mr. Alexander has requested you wait in the lobby. He will be right down."

"Oh, okay." Sterling never had me wait for him before. What was he up to?

A few minutes later, the elevator doors slid open, and Sterling stepped out. He paused as he looked at me, and then a smile spread across his face. "You look stunning. Come, the car is waiting."

"But I thought I was having dinner with you and—"

"You are. The new nanny is upstairs with Georgie, so I'm taking you out."

"The new nanny? Her background check went through?" I asked.

"She was vetted by the agency I hired her through. They came highly recommended, and they are highly rated. The extra background check is to mollify the agency *you* work for, not for me."

I nodded in understanding. "Do I get to meet her?"

Sterling twisted his brow and seemed to think as he led me into the back of his waiting car. "I don't think that's a good idea. If she doesn't know who you are, she can't accidentally tell Peggy Stanholt that you are still seeing us."

I settled into the back of the car and waited for Sterling to sit next to me. "That makes sense."

He slid his arm behind my back and tucked me in close to his side. "You were so nervous this morning. I want to see you, Cecelia. I want you with me and Georgie. I don't want to add to your stress. As long as Georgie is being monitored and this nanny works for me, you won't meet her."

"Should I be jealous? Is she pretty?"

He chuckled. "She looks like a grandmother with short, white hair. You have nothing to worry about."

I leaned against Sterling, and for a moment, I didn't worry about anything. He was fulfilling his responsibility to the baby, he wanted to see me, and he was figuring it all out so that I didn't get in trouble.

This could work. And when he kissed me, I stopped thinking altogether.

He didn't stop kissing me until the car stopped and the back door opened.

"We're here," he said as he climbed out of the car.

I hesitated. We were safe and alone in the car, but outside, people could see us. What if the wrong people did?

He leaned on the open door and ducked down to look at me. "No one you know is going to see you with me here."

"How can you be so sure?"

"The same reason no one was going to see us at the park the other day. Exclusivity. This isn't the kind of place that… Well, let's just say, I doubt any of your coworkers would come here." He held his hand out to me.

"Promise?" I asked as I took his hand. I stepped out of the car and realized he was right. This was the kind of restaurant that celebrities and the super-rich went to, not social workers.

"I'm glad I changed. Coming here in my work clothes would have been awkward."

"You looked fine in what you had on earlier. But I'm glad you changed. I like that dress." Sterling leaned in and whispered, "I can't wait to see it on the floor."

A blush assaulted my cheeks. Sterling laughed as I buried my face against his arm.

"You are adorable when you blush," he said.

"And you're incorrigible for making me blush."

"It's so easy to do," he crooned.

"Sterling." I felt my blush burn bright. "I thought we were supposed to go over some of your lists for Georgie."

"I'm demonstrating my competency," he said with mock-affront. He even placed his hand on his chest dramatically. "I thought you would be impressed that I managed to get a nanny and arrange for us to go out. We can go over lists another time. Come on, let me show you a good time first," he said as he led me into the restaurant. "They even serve realistic food portions here."

"You mean it's not so fancy they can't give anything but a taste?"

He shook his head. "Not nearly as fancy as that, but not so casual that you'll get enough to feed the state of Texas on your plate."

We had food. I barely remembered any of it. It was good, I think. And there was dessert, but it wasn't as interesting or captivating as watching Sterling. I spent the entire time staring at his mouth and his fingers. He smiled and laughed. I kept thinking about how he wanted to see my dress on the floor. I did too, right next to his trousers and shoes.

27

STERLING

I had an entire evening planned, dinner, and then a stroll touring some high-end galleries, but Cecelia kept staring at me, and the way she kept staring at me made me think that maybe we needed to skip everything and go home.

"What's next?" she asked after we had been gazing at each other over an empty table for a while.

"I could continue to charm you and convince you that I am a man of many talents, or…"

"Or?"

"We could skip all of that and I could show you," I practically growled. The need in my chest to get Cecelia alone was feral. It didn't care about nuance and seduction.

To my surprise, she didn't blush. "Dress on floor time?" she asked in all innocence.

My cock surged. It was all I could do not to lunge for her then and there, claim her right now, consequences be damned.

I jumped to my feet and pulled her along with me. The car had better be waiting.

"Sterling." She laughed as she had to run to keep up with my strides.

I practically tossed her into the back of the car when it pulled up. I dove in after her and pulled her against my chest. My mouth found her skin, and I began kissing and sucking and tasting.

"Sterling, you're being a beast." She pushed me back and then made knowing glances toward the front of the car.

"He's not going to care," I growled.

"Maybe not, but I am. No sex in the car. Please."

I ran my hand through my hair and then wrapped my arms around Cecelia's shoulders. "Of course. This is going to be the longest ride home in history," I snarled.

"The nanny!" Cecelia sat up and looked panicked. "She can't see me. I'm not having sex with the nanny at your place."

"We don't have to go to my home. We can go to yours," I suggested.

"Yes!" she exclaimed as if it were a fabulous new idea.

I chuckled. I think she was as muddleheaded as I was right now. All I could think of was how soon I could touch her, and she was trying to figure out where. I gave the driver instructions to her apartment.

Cecelia melted against me, her body, soft and warm, pressed into me. It was torture to not stroke and caress every inch of her. If I started, I wouldn't stop, and I'd promised no sex in the car. I had to be content with her kisses, her wonderful, tempting kisses.

My groin ached long before we made it to her apartment complex.

We both practically ran as soon as the car stopped. Cecelia kept giggling and turning around to make sure I was behind her. As if I were going to let her get away from me. She had her keys out. I took them from her and grabbed her, pressing her against the door as I unlocked it. My lips were on hers, my hands finally roaming over her curves.

The door opened, and I pulled the keys before tossing them on the little table she had. I kicked the door shut and grabbed her again. Or maybe she was grabbing me. Her hands were on me as much as my hands were on her.

She fumbled the buttons of my shirt as I gathered the hem of her dress into my fists and pulled it up. Our lips barely parted as I hauled the dress over her head, and then we were pressed back together, consuming each other in a mutual fire of passion and lust.

I kicked off one shoe and took a few steps before having to pause to pull the other one off. We left a trail of our belongings between the front door and her bed. We crashed together onto the mattress. I rolled with her in my arms as we continued to fight the rest of our clothes off. So much for seduction. I needed her skin against mine.

I shuddered and let out a long breath when her naked breasts grazed my ribs. Yes, this. All of this. I caressed my hands over her smooth back and over the fullness of her hips. I needed more hands, more lips. There wasn't enough of me to get all of her that I craved.

I rolled, pulling Cecelia over me. "I want you where I can see you," I growled.

She perched on my hips, my cock pressed between us. She braced against my shoulders. This was better. I could see her, touch her with my eyes and my hands. Her breasts spilled over, too much bounty for just one hand as I held them, caressed them.

She licked and nibbled her lower lip as I toyed with her nipples between my fingers. She clutched my forearms. Her hips rocked back and forth, slowly at first. Her slick heat glided over my shaft.

I moaned with how good she felt under my touch, how sexy she looked with her half-closed lids and glossy pink lips. She was exquisite torture. I wanted to watch her enjoying the way my touch made her feel. I wanted her wet heat surrounding me. I wanted so much, and I couldn't have it all the way I wanted it. All at once, all the time. I had to portion out the delights of her body. I could not have all of her under my tongue and see the way desire played across her face at the same time.

But I could have her breast in my hands and my fingers deep between her legs. Reluctantly, I let go of one breast and slid my fingers between our bodies until I was diving deep into the folds of her pussy.

Cecelia whimpered and pressed her hips down against my hand. I didn't think either of us was going to last very long. I slipped my fingers inside her. Her inner muscles were already pulsing and sucking with a rhythm that would easily trip over into uncontrolled frenzy with a gentle flick of her clit. I wanted to be inside her for that.

I hated to break the physical connection between us, but if I didn't…

"Are you on birth control?"

"Yeah, why?" She stopped rocking to gaze down at me.

"I don't want to stop for a condom. I want to release into you and fill you with my seed."

"Oh." She shivered with a gasp. She gulped and then nodded. "Yes, fill me. That sounds positively sexy. I like it when you talk like that."

"You mean you want me to tell you I'm going to stretch you out and pump you so full of my cum, you'll be leaking for days?"

Her eyes went wide. Maybe that was too much.

"Yes, say more." Her demand was a low moan that shot straight to my balls.

Holy fuck. She was a complete turn-on. I was more than ready to fill her and explode. Now, my cock was somehow even harder.

"You need to slide that wet pussy of yours onto me now," I demanded.

"Yes," she cried.

I ran circles around her clit with my thumb. "You like that?"

"Uh-huh." Every noise she made was more enticement.

"Pole dance on this." I thrust up into her. She ground down against me.

"Tell me what to do, Sterling."

With her inner walls clenching and pulling at me, I could hardly think. And she wanted me to talk dirty. All I could think was, 'yes, do that, more,' and nothing… my mind was mush as she pulled me into her.

I grabbed onto her hips and held her as I thrust into her. "You are so fucking wet. Like some kind of goddess hovering over me."

I had no idea whether the words coming out of my mouth were coherent or not.

"I'm going to need you to cum for me, baby. Scream for me."

Cecelia was too far gone to be able to respond. "That's it, squeeze my cock. Damn."

I felt her twitch and seize up around me before her orgasm started to flutter and pulse in hard contractions.

I tried to say something along the lines of suck it out of me, but the noise I made as I released it was something more like, "arrggghhhh," incomprehensible garble as I was unable to breathe. And it felt like the heavens opened up and showered me with cotton candy and my favorite vodka. It was sweet and bright and something out of a fever dream. Cecelia's body made me feel all of my favorite things from every point in my life, all at once. She was the thrill of a bungee jump and the exaltation of winning a Lacrosse championship in college. She was the candy store to my inner child, and her body was better than chocolate and the gummy worms I used to be addicted to. She was every good thing that had ever happened, all at once.

Spilling into her wasn't the pinnacle of some physical act of enjoying her body. It was everything all at once. And for the first time in a very long time, I was afraid of what it meant.

.

28

CECELIA

With a stretch that had me pushing off the wall and hanging my feet over the edge of the mattress, I groaned a happy, satiated grumble. I rolled with a flop and draped over Sterling's chest. He was still warm with vestiges of sweat clinging to his chest between his pecs.

Lazily, I trailed my finger through his chest hairs. A sigh of contented bliss escaped me. I was boneless.

One of his hands rested on my butt, the other twisted in my hair.

"You sound like the cat that got the canary," he said.

"Mmm, no. Feathers are too much work. I'm the cat that got warm cream. Hmm. So much warm cream."

Sterling choked as he laughed. "Cecelia, you have a dirty streak. You're all sweet and innocent looking, but underneath it all, you are a vixen."

"Does that bother you?"

He kept touching me, so I guessed not. His entire chest vibrated with his laugh. "Not at all."

I stretched languorously and rubbed against his skin. "What can I say, you inspire me."

He rolled me to the side and then sat up before placing a practically chaste kiss to my lips. "As long as it's something you keep as a treat just for me, it won't bother me at all."

I was limp as he vaulted from the bed. "Where are you going?"

"I'm going to clean up, and then I have to get back. It told the nanny I wasn't going to be out terribly late. It's already ten."

"I wish you could stay," I complained.

"Maybe when this is all settled," he said before he left the room.

I stayed in bed, my eyes closed, enjoying the lingering vibrations and thrums that still tingled across my skin and throughout my core. Sterling's touch was masterful, memorable. I rolled over and propped my chin on my hands, watching him get dressed when he came back in.

"When will I see you again?" he asked.

"Are we talking about this, or do you want me to help you with the baby?"

"That's a ridiculous question, Cecelia. Both."

"We need to coordinate when Peggy is scheduled to be at your place, and when the nanny will be there, so our times don't overlap."

The bed dipped under him as he sat. He ran his hand over my hip and backside. A low hum sounded in his throat. "I have no doubt that you will figure it out. You have exceptional coordination skills."

I crawled into his lap, straddling him. I tugged on his shirt collar and began fastening buttons for him. The fabric of his clothes rasped against my bare skin. As I dressed Sterling, his hands smoothed down my back and over my thighs.

"You are far too tempting to be doing this." His fingers bit into my legs as his mouth claimed mine. The kiss reignited a desperate need deep in my core. I wanted this man so much.

With a moan that sounded pained, he lifted me from his lap and set me on my feet. "I really have to go. Be a good girl."

He kissed me one last time, crushing me against him. I fell back into bed, pouting. I didn't see him out. It wasn't fair. I shouldn't have to choose between him and my job. Especially now that he was no longer my client. Didn't that remove any conflicts of interest?

I lay on my back staring at the ceiling. How was I going to do this? Everything would be so much easier if he would fall in love with me and sweep me off my feet. I could quit my job and move in with him and Georgie. He wouldn't need a nanny, or some agency checking in to make sure Georgie was cared for, because I could take care of her. We could be like a little family.

It was a lovely daydream. But did a man like Sterling Alexander fall in love?

He accepted his responsibilities toward his orphaned niece, but that wasn't the same thing. That was an obligation. I wasn't his responsibility, so why would he keep me around?

I was a good time in bed. At least I hoped I was. I tried. His skills in bed were through the roof, and I was struggling to keep up, anything to keep his interest. No, a man like Sterling Alexander wasn't going to fall in love with me and move me into his apartment to help him raise his ward.

He was going to be interested in me as a distraction and useful help when it came to Georgie. And if that was the best I could get out of him, well, then that's what I was going to cling to.

With a groan of shattered illusions and reality seeping in, I got out of bed and crawled into the shower. I didn't want to wash him off my skin, but I needed to get a grip. I was so far gone in love with the man that I didn't care that I was only being useful to him. Useful in bed, useful in life.

If that's what it took, I was going to be so useful, he would realize he couldn't do without me, and that was kind of like love. Wasn't it? We didn't have to be in love for this to work out, right? One side emotion, the other practicality. As long as I could live with that, I could do this, right?

I got dressed and ran a towel through my hair. It wasn't like I was in a financial position to up and quit my job. But if I got another one, the agency couldn't stop us from seeing each other. If I got another one, would Sterling still be interested in me? Sure, I would still have the same skills, but was the fact that we weren't supposed to be involved part of his attraction to me?

I didn't want to think about that, didn't want to think about all the reasons that could get in the way. I needed to focus on all the ways to make this work. I pulled a notepad from my work tote bag and started to boil water for a cup of tea.

Getting a new job, while an option, wasn't a good one. The job was fine, and I didn't want to think of how hard it would be for Hector's family if I wasn't working on their case. My job wasn't so bad, but finding a new job would be horrible. It had taken me over a year to finally land this one. I didn't want to go back to being a cashier at the craft store.

I liked knowing I was going to have enough in my paycheck to cover rent and have grocery money. If I went back to uncertain hours and an irregular schedule, I'd have to do something desperate, like sell the bag Sterling gave me, just to make sure I had a place to live.

I wasn't willing to do that. That bag was more than just an overpriced tote bag. He had put thought into the gift. He knew I needed it. I glanced at the flip-flop gorilla sculpture. I wasn't going to get rid of that, either. So what if the gifts weren't particularly romantic? They weren't jewelry, but they had meaning for us, for me.

I started a list. I needed to know schedules, mine, the nanny's, and when Peggy planned on checking in on Sterling and Georgie. When did Sterling expect to return to his work? He wasn't going to be on leave forever. How did that impact how we were going to make this work?

Was I expected to just be a glorified nanny? Or did he want actual parenting lessons? Oh, we could take community classes together. The agency couldn't say boo about that. They wanted me to take professional development courses, and he needed some hands-on parenting training. I added the idea to my list and kept brainstorming.

I had more questions than answers, but each question led me toward ideas and strategies I didn't have before. My tea got cold, and I kept writing. At some point, my stomach rumbled, and I was hungry for a snack. Pizza sounded good. It was always a late-night favorite.

When I placed the order for delivery on my phone, I noticed it was much later than I had realized. I had been writing and thinking for hours. It hadn't felt like I had been working that long. I still didn't have any answers, but I felt like I was closer to a solution than I had been hours earlier.

It wasn't until after the pizza was delivered and I had a slice of cheesy pepperoni goodness in my mouth that I thought I might have a solution. Cheesy always did help me think. I frantically scribbled out my ideas before they evaded me.

I thought about calling Sterling with my brilliance but remembered the time. He was essentially a single father with an infant. He'd be asleep. And if he wasn't, he should be. I'd save my good news for the morning. Uh, morning. I still had to go to work in the morning.

Suddenly, all of the adrenaline left over from Sterling's expert lovemaking and the frenzy to find a solution abandoned me. I was exhausted. I dragged myself to bed and fell into a blissful sleep.

2 9

STERLING

y phone buzzed. It was earlier than I expected to hear from Cecelia. I thought she would have still been asleep.

"You're up early," I grumbled. My voice wasn't ready to be awake and functional.

"Sorry, I thought you'd be up with Georgie."

"I am, but she's almost back asleep."

"I woke up, and I am so awake, right now." She sounded entirely too enthusiastic for this time of day.

"You went to bed early," I commented.

"Hardly. After you left, I was up for hours trying to figure all of this out."

"Did you go to bed at all?" I asked.

"I did. And I slept really, really well. I think you had something to do with that."

I was too tired to laugh. I managed a light chuckle. "Happy to be of service."

"You can service me any time," she purred.

"Don't start talking dirty. I'm still under the influence of sleep and am susceptible to your charms."

"Oh, I have charms?"

"You need to stop flirting with me this early in the morning. There is a child present," I gently chastised her. "I do like that you called me first thing, but I am curious as to why."

I could practically hear her blush as she let out a nervous giggle.

"I have a plan that I think will work. I was really afraid we were going to have to wait until Georgie's custody situation was resolved, but... anyway, I wanted to see what the schedule later today looked like. Do you have an appointment with Peggy? What about the nanny?"

"Are you asking if it's safe to come over?"

"That's exactly what I'm asking."

I closed my eyes and thought for a moment. Georgie squirmed and shifted. I opened my eyes to make sure she was okay. Her little head was tilted back, and her mouth fell open with her bottle slowly sliding into the space between us.

"Hold on, let me get the baby back in her bed. Don't go anywhere," I grumbled before putting the phone down.

I lifted Georgie into the crook of my arm. She was getting bigger. Soon, I wouldn't be able to easily carry her with one arm. After tucking her back into her crib, I crawled back into my own bed.

"I'm back," I said with a yawn. "When do you want to come over?"

"Seriously, like right now."

I might have groaned.

"I know I can't, Sterling. I'm just anxious to go over my ideas with you. And to see you again."

"Stanholt and the nanny are scheduled to be here later this morning. No one will be here if you come over for dinner."

"Dinner?"

I made an affirmative grunt.

"If I come by for dinner, how long can I stay?"

"You can stay as long as you want, but maybe plan on leaving by six."

"Six? I won't even be there by six," she complained.

"I meant A.M."

She gasped, and this time, I knew she was blushing.

"I want to hear this plan of yours." I was interested in how she thought it would work. I figured as long as she came over after hours, there was no reason for anyone at her agency to know she was here. And we only had to sneak around for a few months. I'd have to petition the state or something like that for custody, but after all of that was finalized, Cecelia and I could finally go public with our relationship.

I liked that she was organized and had a plan. And that her plan wasn't to simply take care of her, though that wasn't a bad idea. She was too independent to give up her career and take care of me and Georgie. Strong-willed and stubborn. Hmm, and beautiful.

"Come over for dinner. Stay the night," I demanded.

"You don't have to tell me twice. Go back to bed. Sorry I made you talk to me while you were sleepy."

"Don't be silly, Cecelia. I'll see you this evening." I ended the call and slid back into bed. Once upon a time, not so very long ago, before Georgie, I would have taken advantage of being up this early and hit the gym. I groaned and mentally prepared myself to flop onto my back and guilt myself into getting up. Instead, I pushed that stupid idea to the side. Sleep beckoned, and I returned.

The second time I woke up, I almost thought talking to Cecelia had been a dream. But Georgie was in her crib, and her bottle was still on my bedside table. If those things had happened as I remembered, then I accepted that so had talking to Cecelia.

I stayed in the background, not part of the conversation between the new nanny, Mrs. Fletcher—who insisted on being called Nanny Fletcher like some character from a Jane Austin novel—and Ms. Stanholt. They discussed growth milestones and care level expectations regarding Georgie. At no point was my opinion or my participation in the conversation requested.

"I still am her guardian, here," I said at one point.

"Well, of course you are. And you have her best interests at heart. That's all we're discussing," Ms. Stanholt said. I had been summarily dismissed. Only, I was expected to still appear as if I were participating in their discussion.

It was clear to me that the scenarios they were concocting regarding raising Georgie had me out of the picture but footing the bill. That was not going to happen. I grew irritated, and Georgie picked up on my mood and became irritable and cranky.

"I'm going to put her down for a nap," I announced.

When neither woman said anything implying that I needed to be there, I scooped up Georgie. I headed to the kitchen first.

"You want a snack?"

Georgie smacked her lips, making eating motions. I grabbed an applesauce from the cupboard and peeled the foil lid from the individual serving-sized container. I didn't bother to put Georgie in her highchair. I spoon fed her as I carried her back to the bedrooms. I was getting pretty good at this.

It didn't take much to finish off the snack between the two of us.

Georgie yawned and rubbed her eyes. I rocked back and forth on my feet for a bit, soothing her until another yawn split her face. She didn't fight it when I laid her in her crib. I patted her back for a few more minutes until I was certain she was out before I returned to the living room.

Ms. Stanholt looked at me as if I had done something wrong. I was beginning to realize that was pretty much all the time. "You can't just leave with the baby like that," she said.

"Yes, I can. She's my niece, and this is my home. And while I get your agency is concerned that she is cared for properly, I am still the one caring for her."

"That's why Nanny Fletcher is here." Ms. Stanholt pursed her lips and opened her eyes wide at me, as if to make a point.

"Remember, I'm only here part-time until Mr. Alexander returns to his work. Then I'll be full-time."

Nanny Fletcher shot me a quick glance and a wink before returning her undivided attention to Ms. Stanholt and their discussion regarding the proper foods Georgie should be eating and when.

Peggy Stanholt would probably have a nervous breakdown if she knew that more than half the time, I had Georgie eating the same foods I had, and not baby mush.

It seemed forever before Ms. Stanholt announced we were done for the day, like some overly strict teacher dismissing class. I stared at her for a long while before she stood up to leave. I think she may have forgotten this wasn't her office. I let Nanny Fletcher see her to the elevator. After all, it was pretty clear to me that the Stanholt woman no longer thought I was in charge of Georgie's wellbeing.

Nanny Fletcher returned to the living room and sat down. I couldn't read her smile. Was she apologizing? Did she think I was as useless as the other woman thought?

"May I speak frankly?" she asked as she folded her hands on her lap.

I nodded. This was going to be interesting.

"That woman is insufferable."

I barked out a laugh. Tension eased out of my shoulders. What a relief. I wasn't the only one who thought so. "Yeah, yeah, she is. I thought for a while there that you were going to defect to her way of thinking."

"She really doesn't think you have any skill or intention of raising your niece, does she?"

I shook my head.

"The agency she works for originally sent someone over who provided some kind of training. Well, she told me what to do and what to buy. This case manager, she manages the case, not the people involved. Sometimes, I think she forgets that Georgie is an actual person and not a name on a piece of paper," I admitted.

"I think you might be right," Nanny Fletcher said. "Well, I'm sorry I can't stay longer, but I am back tomorrow afternoon."

I saw Nanny Fletcher to the elevator. It was good to know she was more inclined to be on my side. I needed the support and assistance in raising Georgie. And I *would* be raising Georgie.

30

CECELIA

A strange sound infiltrated my dreams. It was squawking, like a giant screeching eagle, or at first, that's what I thought it was. I was being buffeted by the downdraft of large, dark wings. The giant bird in my dream shifted, and somewhere, the transition from dream to sleepy reality happened and the screeching was the baby monitor, and the buffeting was Sterling shifting in and out of bed.

"What?" I asked groggily.

"Shh," Sterling soothed as he climbed back in bed with Georgie in his arms.

I didn't know if he was shushing me or her. She snuggled into the pillows between us. She wrapped her little hand in my hair, her big, expressive eyes locked with mine. She shifted her gaze back and forth a few times between Sterling and me.

She let go of the bottle she was sucking on and had the widest open-mouthed baby grin I think I ever saw on her. No longer interested in relaxing, and possibly going back to sleep, she was up on her feet and climbing around the bed between us.

She giggled and grabbed at my face, planting her version of kisses on me. She only puckered up if someone made the same facial expression at her first. Otherwise, she kissed with the same consuming enthusiasm she approached a cupcake with. Grab, bite, love.

"Is she always like this? What time is it?" I moaned.

Sterling chuckled. "She reminds me of you?"

"What. How? It is rude o'clock in the morning. I'm never awake this early," I said.

"You were yesterday," he reminded me.

"That was past me. Present me would like to be asleep."

"She's just happy to have you in bed with us. I know how she feels." He was gorgeous and sexy, and my insides did a little flip. I loved the way his hair was a mess, and the stubble on his chin was a little thicker and heavier. And his morning voice was deep and rumbly.

"Yeah, but you aren't jumping on me and biting my face."

"No, that was last night. And never with present company." His wicked grin tugged at the corner of his mouth, and I really wanted to kiss him. But he was right, not with Georgie in bed.

I sighed and wanted to fade back to dreamland, but Georgie was entirely too enthusiastic. I needed to get up and go home so I could get ready for work. I very purposefully did not bring work clothes with me so that I would be forced to leave Sterling's bed in a timely fashion.

With great effort, I forced myself to roll onto my side, giving Georgie my back. She thought this was great fun and used me as some kind of springboard. At least that's what it felt like.

"Gotcha," Sterling said. And Georgie giggled.

I sat up and twisted to look at them. My heart clutched at this moment. This wonderful, precious moment of the three of us, sleepy, together. It felt like family. It felt like home. I blinked because I knew what love looked like. This was it.

I didn't want to leave and go to work. My priorities felt all wrong. I really needed to rethink this job. It wasn't fair that I had to choose between work and love, or that I had to be deceptive in order to have both. The night before, I laid everything out for Sterling, how we could make certain that I never was here close to working hours to avoid any possible run-ins with my colleagues, and any date nights, he came to me, so no overlap with the nanny. And on weekends, we could go away.

It was possible to sneak around. And when Georgie was his with full custody and the agency had no more interest or responsibility for her, we could stop sneaking. We could openly be together. Sterling seemed to have liked the plan so much that he carried me to bed to celebrate.

Part of my big plan was that when I did spend the night, I would never leave for work from his place. And that meant this morning. I knew our time was limited. He would have to return to work soon. We didn't talk about it, but standard family medical leave was twelve weeks at the most. He only had about three weeks left.

At that point, I wouldn't be spending work nights with him. I knew this was a rare moment for so many reasons, and I wanted to hold on to it.

"You off?" he asked.

I nodded. A lump in my throat made talking without crying hard. I didn't want to cry in front of Sterling right then.

I got up and got dressed. I returned to his side of the bed to give him and Georgie, who had finally settled down and was looking sleepy, kisses goodbye.

"Are you coming over tonight?" he asked.

I shrugged. "I haven't gotten a whole lot of sleep the past few nights. I think I'm just going to go home after work and go to bed early," I admitted.

"Call me," he said before cupping his hand around my neck and pulling me back for another kiss.

Going home and getting ready for work felt like a chore. I didn't want to go. Maybe my attitude would have been different if I weren't headed into the office first thing. I liked helping my clients. I did not like the antiquated office situation.

I put on my little grey suit and slicked my hair into a bun. I felt like I was donning armor. I didn't expect work to be particularly challenging. I just didn't want to be there. Once there, my bad attitude made me feel worse because I knew it was all mental. I was playing head games with myself. If I could convince myself that I worked for the bad guys, then I could also convince myself that I worked for the good guys.

I stored my stuff away in my desk, pulled out a pad of paper, and made my way into the copier-slash-breakroom. I needed coffee and I needed the report forms.

"Oh, what's this?" I asked no one in particular when I got there and there was a stack of new forms in the slot. They were practically fancy and high-end compared to what we had been using. The forms were already in triplicate. The top sheet was white, and the next two pages were yellow and pink.

I hadn't seen forms like this in a long time. They worked best with typewriters, something we didn't have, and they did not work in printers, which was fine, since I still hadn't been given a laptop.

I was practically giddy. I couldn't be sure if I was actually happy with the forms or just going slightly mad because I had a carbonless form but no real technology to accomplish my job. I took my coffee and a few copies of the form back to my desk.

Greta leaned on my desk looking bored when I got back.

I held up the forms. "We're getting fancy. Any updates on the computer system?"

"We need to chat," she said, completely ignoring my question. She stood up and began walking away.

That was my cue to follow her. So, I did. Her office was suspiciously clean. The surface of her desk was void of the piles of files I was used to seeing. Instead of folders, in the middle of her desk was a folded shirt. It was mine

I reached out and poked the shirt. "How did you get my shirt? I've been missing this for a few weeks." I picked it up and unfolded it, draping it over my arm.

Greta sat and took in a long, deep breath. "Peggy brought that to me."

"Huh?" My brow twisted up with confusion. "How did she get my clothing?"

Greta pursed her lips and looked pained. "She found it at the Alexander residence."

My entire body went cold, and then sweat beaded along my spine. Crap, I hadn't realized I left any clothes at Sterling's. And then I remembered something. I smiled.

"That must have been in the early days when I was showing him how to feed the baby. I took spare clothes because I didn't want to get my good work clothes messy." I indicated my suit.

Greta shook her head. "I don't think so, Cecelia."

I kept my posture perfect and didn't let my expression change. I wasn't going to let Peggy's snooping around in Sterling's things get me fired.

"She said it wasn't there one week, and it was the next," Greta continued.

I did some mental calculations. Peggy had to have been holding on to the shirt for a good two weeks, at least.

"We know you have continued to see Mr. Alexander and the child."

"I thought as case managers, we were supposed to make sure our clients had the tools and supplies they needed, not snoop through their belongings?" was my only response.

31

STERLING

With Georgie asleep, I decided to take the baby monitor and go for a run on the treadmill. I had let the habit of working out slip away as taking care of Georgie had become all-encompassing. How the hell did women do it?

They took care of kids, they worked, they took care of their families, and they had to deal with the pressures of society to return to physically fit conditions. I had help, and I still hadn't managed a regular workout in weeks.

One step at a time. I needed to get myself to some of those parenting classes. Maybe that was where the secrets to being able to manage everything plus a baby were divulged.

The lights flickered. I looked up from my thoughts and saw Wayne waiting for me to acknowledge him. I nodded and stepped off the treadmill, letting the rollers continue.

"Miss Cecelia is on her way up," Wayne announced.

"Really? I didn't expect her today." I shut down the treadmill and grabbed the baby monitor before I followed Wayne upstairs.

It was late afternoon. Far too early for her to come over. She was the one who decided that she wouldn't ever be here when there was even the slightest chance that anyone from her office could be, or the nanny. She had been very specific about that, including how her name should not appear as a contact in my phone, but I should instead use a code or a pet name for her.

She was very specific about covering tracks and not being found out.

I cut through the kitchen and checked my phone where I had left it plugged in and charging to see if she had called or texted and whether I had missed it. Something had to be wrong. My gut twisted. Feeling that things weren't right, I went to check on Georgie, to see if she was okay. She was sound asleep. There was no reason to assume anything was wrong. I just felt the need for reassurance.

Cecelia stormed out of the elevator and was looking around as I approached. She hurled a wadded-up T-shirt at me.

"She's been going through your things!" She looked like she had been crying.

I looked at the shirt in my hand. "Who has been going through my things?"

I lifted the shirt to my nose. It smelled clean, of the fabric softener Wayne used. I didn't understand.

"Peggy Stanholt gave my shirt, that she found here, to my boss. I told her I probably left it here back when I was your case manager, but she didn't believe me. She said they knew I've been seeing you. I never once admitted to anything. But she had information. I think they've had me followed or something."

A growl escaped my throat. I didn't like the thought of someone I was supposed to trust actively spying on me. And I was supposed to trust the agency. After all, they wanted what was best for Georgie. It didn't mean that I did trust them, though.

"Why would they do that?"

Cecelia raged and threw her hands as she paced in a tight circle. "I wish I knew. I mean, fine, they think there is something going on between us, then fire me already. But I don't get the whole point of removing me from the case and then spying on you."

"Are they investigating me?" I asked.

"Not that I know of, but there is something else going on that I am not privy to. I thought they just didn't want me getting too attached."

I started to chuckle, but one look at her face, and the sound died in my throat. Cecelia did not find humor in the irony of that.

"Are you listening to me?" She stopped and glared at me.

"I am listening."

"Then why don't you say something?" she asked.

She was so distressed, she wasn't making sense. How was I supposed to listen and still say something? I had heard her. The Stanholt woman was snooping through my belongings. I already had a list forming in my head of what to do next. I would give the agency a call and request their documentation on a background check and any insurance bonding they had on her. I would request that an internal investigation be made regarding the removal of any other belongings from my home.

I smiled slightly, not because of the extra unnecessary work this situation put me in but because of Cecelia's influence on my life. I was making lists. I could even visualize each step in her loopy handwriting on a sheet of paper.

Pointing out that she was working herself into a frenzy wasn't going to do anyone any favors. "I was thinking about what you said. I am listening, and this puts us at a disadvantage."

"Disadvantage? Sterling, they're transferring me across the state."

"What? Why?" I asked.

She pinched her lips shut and breathed through her nose like a huffing bull ready to charge. "Apparently, it's a temporary transfer, at least for now. They don't even care that I have clients here who will be put at a disadvantage by my absence."

I stared at her, still wrapping my head around what she was telling me. They were spying on me, on us.

"Okay, how temporary?"

She glared at me and stared hard. "They are sending me away!"

"I heard you. Why? Where?" I needed more answers than I was getting.

"You don't look very upset." Cecelia's words were very clipped. She adjusted her shoulders and stood more upright.

"I'm still trying to make sense out of what you are telling me. No, I don't like any of the words you've said so far, but I don't have enough information to be upset yet. Trust me, I will get there." It was hard to keep irritation out of my voice. Cecelia was frantic, and I wasn't keeping up because she wasn't giving me all of the pertinent details.

"I don't have a choice. If I want to keep my job, I have to be there next week. And then they might decide to make it permanent."

I didn't ask, I just lifted my hands in a hopeless gesture. "Where?"

"They're sending me to Amarillo!" she wailed.

And then the baby monitor started wailing. I was surrounded with the sirens of distressed women. Georgie shrieked. I flinched.

"Let me get her." I started to turn to get the baby.

"That's all you're going to say?"

"Cecelia, I have to get the baby," I said evenly.

"Oh, crap. Why did I even bother?" She continued to glare at me as she stepped inside the elevator and punched the buttons.

I was torn between getting Georgie and going after Cecelia. Georgie didn't scream like that. I had to see what was wrong. I was surprised that Cecelia wasn't following me. I turned to watch her step into the elevator.

"Cecelia, that's not what... I meant," But she didn't hear me as the doors closed on my words. I stood there, still, not exactly certain how to respond.

Georgie howled again and I ran down the hallway. "What?" I barked as I crashed into her room.

Her face was red and tear-streaked, and my yell scared another high-pitched scream from her. She tried to get away from me as I approached the crib. She was sweaty and upset, and I had come in like some monster.

"Oh, baby girl, I'm sorry. I'm so sorry." I lifted Georgie into my arms. She was soaking wet. No wonder she was miserable.

My focus shifted. I was very aware that I needed to call Cecelia and explain myself, but right now, Georgie needed me, and Georgie was my priority.

I peeled her wet clothes off and wiped her down with baby wipes. She really needed a bath. I could imagine that it would be a disaster. She was already miserable and upset. Shoving her into a shower wouldn't make her feel any safer. I got her dressed in something clean and dry before I carried her into the kitchen and warmed up a bottle.

It took her a long while to settle. Whatever she had dreamed about had spooked her. Or maybe waking up covered in urine was really that upsetting. She didn't want me to put her down.

With Georgie clinging to me like a baby koala, I found my phone where I had left it in the kitchen and tried to call Cecelia. It went straight to voicemail. I suspected she hadn't even turned the phone on for the day yet, and I doubted she was home.

She was pissed off at me and the world. She needed to calm down before I felt like I could reasonably talk to her. Moving to Amarillo wasn't a bad idea, but only because no one would know who I was there.

I could visit her whenever I had time or wanted, and we wouldn't have to hide. But I hadn't said that. I hadn't responded the way Cecelia had wanted, had needed me to respond. And then I went and barked at the baby.

I kissed Georgie on the head. "I'm sorry," I muttered. I hadn't treated either of my special girls very well.

32

CECELIA

I was numb. The elevator doors closed, and I was alone. I had no feelings. Everything I thought I knew was wrong. A weird, disjointed calmness took over.

Sterling didn't care. I had been willing to risk my job, my career for him, and in return, he just looked at me as if I wasn't speaking English. I wanted to be mad, I wanted to rage and scream and kick. But I felt nothing. I was a little hungry. That's all.

I stopped by a take-out sushi place, got my favorite crab roll and a bowl of miso soup. They wouldn't sell me a beer to-go, so I stopped and picked up a couple of bottles of Sapporo from the convenience store on the way home.

I set up my little dinner. The last time I had gotten sushi was to celebrate getting the job. Was this a celebration of my transfer? Or was I celebrating something else?

My insides twisted. There it was, the regret, the sadness. I took a sip of beer, and my insides settled. No, that was not emotional distress. My body was hungry and telling me to hurry up and feed it.

The sushi was good, the soup still warm, and the cold beers wrapped it all up nicely. I felt accomplished. I was large and in charge but had zero motivation. I scanned my apartment. Letting out a heavy sigh, I got up from the table and began cleaning.

I was going to Amarillo for a temporary placement. That meant that I still needed to keep this place, at least until they let me know I was being transferred permanently. I figured that would come in a week or two. Well, if I was going to be gone for a few weeks, I wanted to make sure I came home to a clean apartment.

I'd clean first, and then I'd pack. I had tonight and tomorrow, and then I'd drive up. I needed to be in the office there first thing on Monday. I wasn't given an opportunity to summarize my case notes on Hector. I had to hand over the files immediately.

Greta had sat in her chair in her office and told me to bring everything to her immediately. I still had that stupid shirt in my hands when I walked out of her office. I moved like a zombie, or maybe a puppet was a better description. I was doing what I was told to do and not taking steps of my own accord.

"I haven't had a chance to write down today's update," I said when I got back to her office, file folder clutched in my arms.

"That will have to be okay," she said. She held up a slip of paper. "This is the property manager's number and the address of the company-owned apartment you'll be staying at."

I put the file folder down and took the piece of paper.

"Corporate apartment?"

"Yes, we need you there for the week. If we decide to transfer you, of course, at that point, you'll be expected to be responsible for your own housing."

"I have a lease. I can't afford to break it," I pointed out.

"Relocation services will negotiate getting you out of that if necessary. And they'll cover the expense as the cost of moving. You'll be given a moving allowance."

Shock had rolled in about that time. "But what if I don't want to move to Amarillo?"

"You want to keep your job, don't you?"

"Yes, ma'am." And suddenly, I was the naughty child, and this was my punishment. And it was the worst possible of all outcomes. In that moment, I felt the overwhelming weight of every mistake I had ever made in my entire life.

In full pain and panic mode, I instinctually went to Sterling. His rejection was a deeper shock, and I could no longer feel or care about anything. Now, hours later, it was an effort to shrug and think anything more significant than *whatever*.

I used my toothbrush to deep clean the grout between the tiles on the tub surround. It wasn't like I was going to move with an old toothbrush. I was more invested in the results of scrubbing the tub and the toilet in my bathroom than what was going on in my life.

It was late when I finally felt that the apartment was properly cleaned. I stood in the middle of my living room and looked around. What was I supposed to do now? I didn't want to sit down and mess up the throw pillow organization I had done.

My tummy rumbled again. I ran my hand over it, hoping it would settle down. Maybe I was hungry? I looked at the time. It was late. Deciding bed was the thing to do, I could figure out what to do with the food in the refrigerator in the morning.

The actions I took were logical steps. I felt completely disconnected from any of the decisions I made. I didn't dream, and I woke up feeling functional about nine hours later. I was already in trouble with work. What were they going to do? Fire me? I wanted to say goodbye to Lucille and Hector. It also was a way for me to clean out my refrigerator. Just about two hours later, I stood on Lucille's front porch holding a box of everything from my refrigerator and a good portion of the canned goods from my pantry.

"Cecelia? What are you doing here this morning? We don't have an appointment."

"Yeah, I'm sorry to take up your time. I wanted to let you know that I'm being transferred, and I won't be your case manager any longer. I don't know who they have taking over for me. I hope it's okay, but I thought of you when I realized I needed to clean out my freezer. I know you've been struggling, feeling like you're always behind schedule, and that groceries have been a challenge."

"Come in." Lucille stepped back, and I stepped in, carrying my box to the kitchen.

"I also wanted to say goodbye to Hector. I wanted to tell you myself. I didn't want you to think I was abandoning you." The words sounded more emotional than I felt.

"They called us yesterday. But thank you for coming over yourself. This will mean a lot to Hector."

I followed her to his room. I kneeled down next to his bed and spoke softly. I squeezed his hand, and he looked sad. I felt bad for hurting his feelings. And I felt confused when Lucille hugged me just before I left. Maybe if I had some semblance of emotion, I would have felt sad too. As it was, I went through the motions. I returned Lucille's hug, I ruffled Hector's hair. It looked like I cared.

I didn't care about anything. I was functioning. On the way home, I stopped and got an oil change and had my tires checked. I had a long drive ahead of me.

I packed, leaving behind the gifts from Sterling that wouldn't be appropriate anyway. My car was ready. I went to bed early and woke up at dawn. Amarillo was only about a six-hour drive, but I needed to be there in a timely fashion to be let into the apartment.

* * *

I wasn't fully aware of everything I did, and then, I found myself standing in the middle of a soulless apartment with an old Naugahyde couch from the previous century. It was as if I woke up, or a fog cleared. I became aware of everything. My skin hurt. My hair would have been screaming if it could. My stomach roiled, and I struggled to breathe. The pain and loss of everyone was so sharp and fresh. My very soul felt slashed and bleeding.

My sobs were deep, gut-wrenching things that pulled anguish up from my very toes. I collapsed in on myself and folded into a ball in the middle of that wretched apartment in a sketchy building in a questionable part of town.

I didn't want to be there. I didn't want to be alone. Why had everyone turned on me? My job, Sterling?

It felt as if Lucille, my client, had been my only friend and I had felt nothing as I left her and her broken little child with a 'there-there', distracted pat on the back.

I cried until I needed to throw up. And then I cried even more. I managed to crawl into the bedroom. The bed needed to be made. The mattress was inside a plastic zipped bag. Mattresses in plastic bags were never a good sign. But that didn't stop me from curling into the middle of it and crying myself to sleep.

I woke up stiff and feeling sick. Monday morning, and I was expected in the local office. I dragged myself through all the tasks of getting ready for work.

I looked for coffee in the kitchen and decided I wasn't going to use anything in there until I had time to do a top to bottom disinfecting scrub-down. Everything about the apartment seemed to need a thorough scrubbing. I didn't know if I had it in me or not. I cursed as I slammed cupboard doors closed during my search for cleaning supplies. I was going to need to make a list of everything I needed. Looking at the time, I groaned. Not that I wanted to go to work or clean this place, but I had to be in the office soon, and I didn't know what the traffic was like in the town on a Monday morning.

33

STERLING

week later...

"Fuck!" I threw my phone across the room. I ran my hand through my hair and squeezed my temples together. This past week had not been going well. I was arguing with the agency that was supposed to be helping me figure out how to care for a child. Their case manager had crossed a line, and now they were threatening to take Georgie from me.

And the one person I had thought was on my side from the very beginning, at least she had acted like she was, well, she wasn't returning my calls. I was pretty sure I'd fucked things up with her. So, not a good week, and not a good time to hear possibly the worst news of my life delivered in a snooty, self-righteous voice.

Wayne crossed the far side of the living room and picked up my phone. He held it out to me as he crossed in my direction.

"Bad news?"

I growled. "Very. That was the director of the agency. They are waiting on confirmation, but it appears that Georgie's father may have been found."

"I thought that was always the goal?" he asked.

I barked out a sardonic laugh. "That hasn't been the goal for a while. I don't want her father to be found. I want to keep her."

"She is not some puppy who followed you home, and now the rightful owner has shown up—"

"No, she's not. She is Argene's daughter." I clenched my teeth and felt the muscle in my jaw tense and pulse. I wasn't going to explain it to him. I tried to explain it to the next case worker who was sent my way after I refused to let Peggy Stanholt into my home—she had violated a trust. She wasn't welcome. I told them to send someone else. They did. I had almost hoped they sent Cecelia back.

Fuck!

The only person who seemed to understand my need to protect Georgie when I failed her mother was Cecelia. She hadn't returned a single call all week. I knew she had relocated to Amarillo for a short-term transfer. But hadn't she taken the phone I bought with her?

I took the phone from Wayne. I stared at it. What should I do next? Who should I call first? I wasn't used to being in a position of uncertainty. I made executive decisions that made people, especially myself, lots of money. Georgie wasn't a fluctuating market or an old tech process that needed to be disrupted.

I hit the number for the guy I had looking for Georgie's father.

He answered on the first ring.

"That's bullshit," he said when I reported that the other group claimed to have located him. "If this guy exists, I would have found him by now. I've combed through your sister's contacts. I've chased down everyone in every picture she posted to her social media in a four-month window around what would have been time of conception.

Half of those people she called friends don't even remember her. And the ones who did had no idea she had gotten pregnant. I can tell you she was bouncing between Miami and the islands. Your sister partied. I'm good, but not even I can track down every single person who was at the same parties she went to during that time."

Why the hell had Argene made that request? Why not just grant me custody? Why play this game that there was a father out there who might want his child?

"Tell you what I'm gonna do. I'll put a trace request on the kid's genetic records. That way, I'll get a ping if anyone with any kind of close match comes up."

"What if they aren't using the same database?" I grumbled.

The PI barked out a laugh. "It's all the same database. If they get a match, I'll know about it. In the meantime, make sure they aren't trying to play you somehow."

"Play me?"

"Yeah, you know, like tell you they got the dad and have you sign over custody papers. The kid then gets adopted out for big bucks. Especially one as cute as what you got."

A chill like ice cubes ran down my spine. "Keep me posted."

I ended the call and immediately called my lawyer. It took several minutes of being put on hold and being transferred, and on hold again, before I got to my lawyer, Paul Chavez.

"Can you get a subpoena or a warrant or whatever so that the agency has to disclose who their investigators are and what they have found?"

"You want me to go in front of a judge to request their records be disclosed?"

"Yes, that's exactly what I want," I said.

"It's not going to be cheap," Chavez said.

"I can afford it. Look, they said they might have a lead on Georgie's father. They won't share their findings with my guy, and when I checked in with him, he told me it sounds fishy." As I proceeded to share with Chavez what the PI said, I sounded paranoid. But this was Georgie I was talking about. I wasn't going to stop being suspicious until I was awarded full custody.

"Normally, I would say he's making shit up, but there have been similar cases in the past. Kids get 'lost' in the system, only to find out someone in DCS pocketed a lot of adoption fees. And you mentioned last week, they were snooping through your laundry and belongings. Do you trust your nanny? She's not going to hand over the kid if these people show up saying they have her father some time when you aren't around?"

I didn't like the sound of that. "Yeah, I think so. She's not one of theirs."

"Huh?"

"They tried to get me to hire from a nanny place they recommended. I didn't like their recommendations. I found my own," I admitted.

"I would sit down with your nanny and lay it out. Tell her your concerns and that under no circumstances is she to hand that baby over to anyone not yourself, even if the kid's father miraculously turns up on your doorstep crying about how he's been looking for her for months."

None of this would be a concern if they had just let Cecelia stay as my case worker. There was no way she would have ever been involved in a plot to take Georgie away from me.

The baby monitor sounded with Georgie's babbles as she woke up from a nap. She wasn't crying or distressed, so I let her be while I finished my call with Chavez.

I didn't feel relaxed or confident after either call. I punched Cecelia's number. It went straight to voicemail. "You've got your reasons. I'm trying to understand. Something concerning has come up with your employers and Georgie. I think they got you out of the way. Give me your address. I want to come see you."

I pulled up the photo of Cecelia, Georgie, and me. It had been the day I knew she belonged with me, both of them. She was all smiles, and her yellow top coordinated with Georgie's yellow dress and hat. I hadn't even realized I had changed to match them.

Georgie sat playing in her crib, a welcome relief from the times she woke up terrified, miserable, and screaming. When she saw me, she pulled herself up and held onto the rails and said "Dada," a bunch of times.

As I picked her up, my phone slipped into the crib. Georgie managed to pick it up. She looked at the picture and said, "Mama, Dada," and then slobbered all over it in her style of kiss.

My heart, what there was of it and its capacity to hold emotion other than duty and responsibility, shattered. Georgie missed Cecelia as much as I did. I had to accept that I didn't own Cecelia. I thought of her as mine because I loved her, needed her.

The same reason I didn't want Georgie's father to be found. I loved her. Yes, I had a sense of guilt-driven duty to protect her. But I wanted to keep her around and see what kind of kid she became because I loved her. I picked up the little girl I wanted to be a father to and held her until she squirmed.

"Be that way." I chuckled.

Georgie babbled her baby talk. I changed her and then carried her to the kitchen for a snack. I buckled her into her highchair before I started poking around the cupboards.

"Do you need anything, Mr. Sterling?" Wayne asked.

"A snack. Georgie needs something, and I'm kind of hungry too. And I still needed to call and have a discussion with Nanny Fletcher regarding Georgie's safety. And I want to find Cecelia," I said.

"I can help with the snack. What do you mean regarding Georgie's safety?" he asked.

"The PI, and Chavez agrees, says the people at the agency are acting fishy. I'm probably being paranoid, but I need to make sure that no one shows up at the door and says they're Georgie's father and expects anyone here to just hand her over. If the man is found, there will be lawyers and DNA confirmations in place."

Wayne pulled out a box of applesauce servings. He opened it and handed me two applesauces. He turned and pulled a couple of spoons out of the drawer.

"You can count on me to ensure her safety. As far as finding Miss Cecelia, why don't you ask the private investigator who is working to locate Georgie's father? At least with Miss Cecelia, you know her name, her whereabouts, and her employer."

34

CECELIA

hree weeks later...

The temporary transfer to the Amarillo office was dragging out. They couldn't seem to decide whether I was a permanent transfer or if I was simply there as a disciplinary action. And it was all the worse because, while I lived in their corporate apartment, I still paid rent in Dallas.

My life was on hold. Because I had no private time. Since I lived in their apartment, it meant I had to share when other people came to visit this branch of the office. I had my own room, but the bathroom was shared, as was the kitchen. Other people were messy, and they left the place a mess, like this was some kind of hotel. I was tired of cleaning up after people, especially after how much work it had been to get the place clean enough that I was willing to stay.

The Amarillo office was a bit better when it came to work. I wasn't given any cases. Instead, I was given stacks of files with handwritten notes and told to do data entry. Fine. It's actually what I thought I was going to be doing when they first hired me. I had a cubicle with walls that provided a modicum of privacy. That was an improvement over the Dallas office.

And I had a computer. Not the laptop I had originally been told I would have, but I was no longer a case manager, so it made sense. I didn't need a laptop if all my work could be done from a desk. But I didn't like the work, and it felt like everyone knew why I was there. I was treated like some pariah, unwanted, not trusted.

My fingers hurt, and I had started wearing wrist braces. All the transcription work was not being friendly to my wrists. Ten minutes after five, I signed off the server and shut my computer down. If I signed off the server five minutes earlier, someone would show up at my cube the next day and tell me how they really needed me to be a team player. It didn't take long for me to figure out 'team player' was code speak for working longer than the time your job hours are for. Sign in five minutes early, don't take a full hour for lunch, and stay at least ten minutes late.

Fine. I could play that game. They wanted about what looked like twenty extra minutes of work a day out of me. That added up to almost two free hours a week. Over the course of a year, that impacted my income a lot. I reclaimed my time. I didn't sign off the server for coffee or bathroom breaks. At this point, if they fired me, I'd thank them.

After work, I headed to the local library. I didn't have a computer to work on at the apartment, and even if I did, it would be a company machine. I didn't want to use their equipment to look for a new job. And I didn't want to do it while another company flunky was staying in the apartment.

So far, I was the only one who stayed more than one week in a row. I was beginning to wonder if my three roommates so far had really only been working in the local office for temporary reasons, or in town for meetings, or if they saw what was going on and left. I didn't feel like I could leave without an escape plan.

I wanted to go back to Dallas. But I needed a job.

I got tacos from a local food truck. The food was good, and I ate there more than I cooked. There were better tacos in Dallas, but if I were going to miss anything from my time in Amarillo, it was going to be that food truck.

I ate in my car in the parking lot of the library. My stomach complained. It had been doing that more and more. I rummaged around and pulled out the bottle of Tums I'd started carrying in my tote bag. I looked at it as some kind of status symbol of what my life had become. I was so stressed, I had to carry antacids with me.

My stomach lurched again, and this time, I was out of the car and hurrying toward a garbage can. I lost my dinner. That had also been happening more and more. I needed to change something soon, or the stress was going to make me so sick, I'd have no choice.

I returned to my car, thankful everything was still there, even though I had left the door wide open. I opened the trunk and pulled out a warm bottle of water. I used it to wash my mouth out before I popped in the chalky antacids. My stomach complained, but I didn't throw up this time.

I locked the car up and headed inside. I groaned with defeat. The bank of library computers was all full. I grabbed a romance novel from a display and found a nearby chair where I could stake out the computers. I was there for about an hour, and the book was just getting good when a computer opened up and I could sign up.

I kept the novel next to me so I would remember to check it out before I left. In the book, the sassy, quirky heroine ran her own business, and of course, the hot, shirtless yard guy working on her elderly neighbor's house ended up being the neighbor's hot grandson and the sassy heroine's direct business competitor.

I couldn't wait to see how they worked things out and realized they would be even more successful by merging the businesses. If only real life worked out so easily. I didn't run a business, and I had a degree that was pretty much geared toward working in the public sector. But I wanted to afford rent and my car payments. That's how I ended up with a private agency. They simply paid better.

The same three jobs that I applied for the previous week were recommended to me again. This was frustrating. I either was going to have to search for a job outside of my training and interests or I was going to have to consider locations other than Dallas.

I had spent my entire life looking forward to moving to Dallas when I grew up. I wanted to be in Dallas over any other city in Texas. I didn't want to be anywhere else. I didn't want to be in Amarillo. And I really didn't want to relocate to Houston.

I spent as much time as I could on the computer before my stomach decided to betray me once more. I accepted defeat, checked out the book, and headed back to the apartment. There was some woman there who hadn't been there earlier. Another new roomie.

She stepped out of my room. "You wouldn't mind switching rooms with me, would you? This one is—"

"What are you doing in my room?" I demanded.

"I was just looking around. They said another temp was staying here. But I like this room better," she said, pointing into my bedroom.

I let out a long sigh.

"That's my room. I'm not switching."

"You aren't very hospitable," she complained.

I walked past her and into my room. "You're right, I'm not. Complain to whoever you need to, but this is my room. I was here first, and I'll be here after you leave." I closed the door behind me.

I didn't even get her name that first night. She watched TV entirely too loudly, but I had my revenge. The tacos I had for dinner staged another revolt, and I spent most of the night throwing up. I know she heard me because she complained about it.

In the morning, I texted my boss to explain why I would be late. Food poisoning. I waited until after my roommate left to shower and get ready for work. She left the bathroom a mess. Her makeup and feminine hygiene products were everywhere. She must have never lived with a roommate before.

So far, she was a nightmare, and I didn't even know her name.

I tried to neatly move her things aside so I could use the sink. I didn't want her blaming me if her makeup got ruined. I picked up the box of tampons and stopped. Tampons. How had I not needed to buy any of these since I had been in Amarillo?

I tried to calculate when my period was. I couldn't remember last month. I thought I was due for one the week I moved. But... No, it was just stress messing with my body.

But I had been throwing up off and on for at least two weeks now. There was no way I kept getting food poisoning from the taco truck. Their food was too good. If it was bad, I wouldn't crave it so much.

I set the box down on the counter.

I had cravings.

Oh, shit. I was going to need to be even later for work. I had to go buy a pregnancy test and cross my fingers that I failed it.

STERLING

A *week later...*

"This place is a dump," I said as I pulled into the apartment complex where Cecelia was living. I pulled the SUV over into a guest parking space and checked the address the PI texted to me.

It was the right place. Apartment 3A, ground floor, back. The complex was one of those made up of several long two-story buildings arranged in a U-shape. There were two clusters of those, making up two public courtyards. Apartments lined the inner side of the U, and some were located along the outside. The walkways and stairs were along the outside of her building.

I navigated the car around the side of the building where her apartment should be. I recognized her car and parked next to it. I unfastened Georgie's car seat and carried it with me. She was asleep. It had been a long ride.

I spent most of the time talking to her, letting her know what we were up to. I had continued to talk, mostly to myself but out loud, even after I knew she had fallen asleep.

I found apartment 3A and knocked. I stepped back so that if Cecelia looked out the window or through a peephole in the door, she would be able to see me clearly. Nerves I hadn't expected or experienced in a very long time made me antsy.

The door opened. A woman with a purse hooked over her shoulder answered the door. She was dressed to go clubbing in a short form-fitting dress and towering heels. Her hair was slicked back, and her jewelry was oversized. She started when she first saw me, then she scanned me up and down like she was checking me out. "Who are you?" She leaned against the open doorjamb.

"I was told Cecelia Harrison lives here."

I stepped back, giving this unknown person room when she took a step toward me. She wiggled her hips from side to side and flipped her hand over her shoulder. She rolled her eyes. "Her? Yeah, she's in there."

She sashayed away, leaving the door open.

"Don't just leave the door open! Jeez, who the hell is it?" I heard Cecelia call out from inside the apartment. "I fucking hate this place."

"Cecelia?" I called out before stepping inside.

The apartment was dark with just the flicker of the TV. It took my eyes a moment to adjust.

"Sterling?" she asked as she uncurled from a pile of blankets on the couch.

"Cecelia." After I closed the front door, I put Georgie's car seat down and went to her, arms outstretched.

She came to me, and then I had her in my arms. She clutched me with desperation.

I peppered her hair with kisses and smoothed my hand over her head and shoulders. She shook in my arms. I knew she was crying.

"I've got you, I've got you now. It will be okay." Cecelia clutched my arms and looked up into my face. Hers was streaked with tears.

"What are you doing here?"

"I came looking for you. You just left," I said.

"I thought you didn't care. I had to leave. They made me come here for the job." She took in a shaky breath.

Guiding her back to the couch, I pulled her down with me so that I could continue to hold her. She settled in against my chest. I held her for a long, quiet moment. My heart settled, finally at peace at having her back where she belonged.

And then she hit me. It wasn't a hard hit, but she slapped her hand against my chest. "You made me think I was crazy and that you wanted to break up. Why didn't you say anything? You just let me leave." She sat up and wiped the tears from her cheeks.

I reached out to wipe away her tears, and she swatted at my hand like an angry cat.

"I'm sorry about that." I closed my eyes and searched for the right words. "I messed up. You were upset, and then Georgie was screaming. I didn't know what to do. I was going to make the wrong move no matter what I did. By not doing anything, I still made the wrong move. You were hurt and angry. And you dropped a couple of bombs on me. You thought Peggy Stanholt was spying on me, on us. And you were moving. My brain latched onto your moving when Georgie started screaming."

Cecelia wiped her face again and pushed off the couch. She crossed the small living room and crouched down to look at Georgie.

"I missed you, baby," Cecelia said softly. She looked over at me. "I missed you too."

"I've been miserable," I admitted. "Have you been here the entire time? Did you come back to Dallas at all?"

She shook her head. "I closed up my apartment, expecting to have to pack up and move. But they keep stringing me along. And as long as they are giving me a place to live, I guess this is what I'm doing for now."

"You don't want to be here," I said.

She shrugged. "I don't have much of a choice right now. And no, I don't. But job leads are scarce, and I need a job with benefits right now. I can't just go back to being a cashier."

"Why?"

She glared at me.

"No, sorry, stupid question. Yes, insurance is important. I figured you left your phone back in Dallas, then?"

Cecelia nodded. "And my bag. At first, I thought that had been dumb. It's a good bag. But with the roommate I've had this week, I'm glad I didn't bring anything valuable. I don't trust her. But yeah. The phone and all that are back at my place in Dallas. Why?"

"I've only left you about a million voicemails. I fucked up, Cecelia. It didn't take me too long to figure that out. But you never returned any of my calls. All I knew is you were in Amarillo. It's not like the director of your office would tell me where you went."

"How did you find me?" she asked.

"The PI I've got looking for Georgie's father. It took him about three days once I called him. But then I had to stick around for another few days. Long story short, I'm suing the agency for lack of disclosure. I suspect they are playing games that will endanger Georgie."

Her head snapped up. "What?"

"After you left, I complained that Peggy Stanholt had overstepped her position as a case manager. She had no right to snoop through my belongings. She violated my trust, and probably some laws. I've got my lawyer on that. Then about a week or so after that, they told me they found Georgie's father."

"No," Cecelia said in a long, drawn-out word. "They couldn't have. I'm so sorry." She knew how I felt about Georgie. She knew that Georgie's biological father showing up was devastating.

"Yeah. I called to chew out my guy. He was supposed to be one of the best. He told me there was no way they found the father when he couldn't. And then he planted an idea that at first seemed paranoid. But after I mentioned it to my lawyer, I'm not so sure it was paranoid. We immediately began taking precautions. That took some time."

"What does that mean?" Cecelia sat on the floor next to the car seat. Georgie was still asleep.

"It means I only want people I can trust near Georgie."

"I can't be your case worker, Sterling."

"I don't want you to be my caseworker. I want you. I am here because of what's going on, but not why you think. As it dawned on me that someone might want to take Georgie from me, I also realized they were taking you from me. They had taken you from me."

Cecelia gulped, and tears started flowing down her cheeks again.

"I want you back, Cecelia. I miss you. Georgie misses you."

She glanced over at the baby. "She doesn't know I'm gone."

I stood and hovered over them. "She does. She looks at your picture and…" I took a deep breath.

Cecelia blinked up at me. Her eyes were bright with the remnants of tears. She put her hand on my leg.

My body surged in response. Her hand against me tightened in my gut. My pulse was far from settled.

I lowered to be close to her. I brushed a stray, random hair away from her brow.

"Georgie looks at your pictures, because I show her them. She gives them slobbery baby kisses, and she calls you Mama."

Cecelia gasped and covered her mouth. She looked from me to the baby and back.

"Oh, baby. Sterling?" She reached out for me.

I pulled her to me. "Come back to us, to me. You belong with us."

Her answer was a kiss.

36

CECELIA

Sterling came for me. His lips were home and his arms my secure shelter. I had felt so lost and alone, and he was here now.

"I couldn't even think after I thought you were breaking up with me. I hurt so completely. It hurts every day," I confessed when his lips left mine.

"Shh, Cecelia, shh. I'm here. We're together. Everything will work out, I promise. Come, stay with me and Georgie tonight. We'll all be together like we are meant to be." He hooked his finger under my chin and looked deep into my eyes.

I missed his deep, earnest expression when he was being caring and thoughtful. I had missed him so much.

I nodded. There was no way they could stay here, not with Reina. She had been here a week, and I had found her in my room more than once. I was really glad I had only packed the basics and we weren't the same size. I did not trust her not to take my clothes or anything she wanted.

"Get me out of here. I hate this place so much," I whined.

"Tell me what you need. Let's get your things. You're coming with me right now," he said.

I loved it when he took charge. I felt safe with him.

"You aren't driving back to Dallas tonight, are you?"

He shook his head. "Not with Georgie. If it was just us, maybe. Let's get your things, and then we can find a hotel for the night."

I pointed into my room. "That's my room. Grab my clothes. I'll get my things from the bathroom."

I stopped and looked at the mess Reina left as she was getting ready to go out. I groaned. I really did not like her.

I grabbed my stuff out of the shower. The new bottle of conditioner was suspiciously light. Screw her, she was using my stuff. Too bad there was nothing of hers that I liked enough to consider taking with me. But I was feeling petty. I left the shampoo and conditioner after I dumped them down the drain and put about an inch of water in the bottles.

I stepped into my room, and Sterling was going through all of the empty drawers. "Is this all you packed?" He gestured to the small pile of clothes on the bed.

"I didn't think I was going to be here for more than two weeks, so I didn't pack much. The complex has decent laundry facilities, so I just wash and wear what I've got." I grabbed my clothes and shoved them into the small bag I had originally packed everything in. I grabbed the library book off the bedside table. "Ready."

Sterling led the way out of the room. He scanned his gaze around the apartment. "Anything else yours?"

I shrugged. "The mess. But Reina can deal with it. I've had to put up with her sloppiness."

I followed him out of the apartment. I stopped when he beeped to unlock a giant Cadillac SUV.

"I should have guessed you drove a car like this. This or a tiny little sports car," I said as I tossed my bag into the back seat.

"You've seen my car before," he said.

I shook my head. "Nope, anytime I've been with you in a car, it's been a car service or a limo."

"There are so many more interesting things to do than drive. But yes, this is my car. I'm too tall for most sports cars."

It made sense. He was tall. Those tiny little cars would require him to fold up on himself. It couldn't be comfortable.

I sighed and closed my eyes as he pulled away from the apartment. I hadn't left a note for Reina. I was a bad roommate. I didn't care. She was a worse roommate. Sterling drove, and a few minutes later, he pulled into a hotel parking lot. I waited in the car with Georgie. She was out cold. Sound asleep.

He climbed back in and handed me a card key. He parked, and we went inside.

The room was a basic nice hotel room. It felt clean in a way I could never get that apartment to feel. I flopped onto the big king-sized bed.

About five minutes later, there was a knock on the door.

"Who's that?" I asked as I sat up. I began pulling my shoes off.

A moment later, someone rolled in a crib. Sterling pointed to an empty spot for it. He handed the bellhop a tip, and we were alone again. He unfastened Georgie, and my heart thrummed just watching how careful he was with her as he put her into the crib. When I first met him, he had been insufferable with a cocktail and leaving her on the floor, and now, he was the best father that little girl could have.

He climbed onto the bed and pulled me against him. We lay like that, just holding each other for the longest time. His hand brushed over my back and shoulder.

I couldn't help it. I had Sterling in my arms. I let my hands roam over his body, feeling the shape of his muscles through his clothes. He let out a soft moan and eased me back onto the mattress before covering me with his length and kissing me.

His lips were tender and warm, and kissing him was the singular best thing that had happened to me in at least a month. His hand skimmed over my ribs before cupping a breast.

I lifted my leg over his and shifted, pressing my hips tighter to his.

With a groan, he pushed away and climbed out of bed.

"Hey," I complained.

"Here we go," was all he said as he unlocked the wheels on the crib and rolled it into the bathroom.

"Did you just put Georgie in the bathroom?" I asked.

"I'm not making love to you with her in the same room. It's not right. And there is no way I am not making love to you tonight."

I gulped at the sincerity and ferocity of his words. I nodded. I wanted him to make love to me too. I wanted his touch to reassure me that everything was going to be okay. I pulled at my clothes in a most functional fashion. I wanted them off. I didn't care about putting on a show. The sooner I could have Sterling's skin against mine, the better.

We pulled the blankets back and slid in against the clean sheets at the same time. I wiggled up against him. His cock pressed against my belly, hard and ready. I was ready too, but I still wanted all the touching and the teasing. Foreplay wasn't just for my body. It made everything feel so much better and gave me more time touching him.

His mouth searched out, placing kisses along my skin until he found my nipple. I mewled and tried to keep the noise down. But it was hard when he made me want to cheer and be loud.

His hands roamed and grabbed at me like he had missed touching me as much as I had missed him. I tugged his hair until he lifted his mouth back to mine. His arms enfolded me, and his lips claimed mine. I was surrounded by him, his body, his warmth, his smell.

This felt like home. It didn't matter where we were as long as we were together. Okay, and maybe not back at that horrible apartment. But I probably would have been happy to have been with him there as long as I was with him.

"Are you good if I don't have a condom?" he murmured against my ear.

"Ah, yeah, I'm good." There was something I desperately needed to tell him, but right now was not the moment. He wasn't going to get me pregnant tonight.

I let out a long sigh when he slid into me. This was the most perfect moment. Each and every time felt like perfection. I belonged to him, and he belonged to me. When we moved together, the world fell away, and we were all that was left.

How could I have doubted this? Brains and emotions got in the way of something so perfect. But that didn't matter now. Sterling slid inside me, and he was where he belonged. I moaned as my body responded. His touch was everything, yet it somehow wasn't enough. I needed more of him, more of his body.

"More," I moaned.

He growled low in his throat. "Demanding."

"More," I whined. I grabbed at his skin, clutching him to me. I bucked my hips up to meet his. "More!"

His mouth over mine stopped my demands. But my body pushed back, and I moved against him. His thrusts grew more forceful, and I took everything he gave me. Everything tightened up. My breathing grew shallower. I was fighting as everything rolled and crashed and sent me over the edge. The orgasm didn't slam into me, it grew and built and became more intense with each touch, each stroke. It made its presence known and then became more and more intense.

I cried out because there was no way I could contain what was in my body. And then I broke apart. I was stardust, I was glitter. I was magic. And then I was me, in Sterling's arms. And I was happy.

He pressed hard against me, grabbing my leg to hold it over his hip. He thrust a few more times before falling to his side. He wrapped his arms around me and kept me tight in his embrace.

"Never doubt that I need you." His voice was gravelly and low as he panted out the words.

I wanted to tell him I loved him, but I think our bodies had conveyed that pretty well.

37

STERLING

Cecelia's skin was soft and warm. I loved touching her, but I couldn't get enough of her. I don't know if I slept or if I just stroked her skin all night as she slept in my arms.

Georgie started to wake up. I didn't need a baby monitor to hear her. She was all of six feet from the end of the bed. I slipped out from between the warm sheets and pulled on my lounge pants. I leaned back over and gently woke Cecelia up.

"Georgie is about to wake up and join us. Get dressed."

"Hmm?" She rolled over and a spray of hair covered her face. She brushed it away and barely opened her eyes to look at me. She was smiling. I was smiling too. It was good to have her back. "Oh, right, baby. She's still asleep."

"I know, but she won't be soon. Throw something on, and you can go back to bed."

She rolled out of bed and grabbed her bag before disappearing into the bathroom. She was a delight to watch. All those curves, and they were mine.

While Cecelia was changing in the bathroom, I prepped Georgie's bottle, and while she was still asleep, I carefully changed her. Over the past couple of weeks, I discovered if I woke up before she did and I could get her comfortable before she fully woke up, she'd stay asleep. I still lost some sleep, but not nearly as much as if Georgie fully woke.

I had her back in the crib and was softly patting her back. She hadn't even needed the bottle. I lifted my finger to my lips when Cecelia emerged in a T-shirt and pair of shorts. She nodded and crawled back into bed. When I was convinced that Georgie was truly back to sleep, I put the bottle in the mini-fridge and climbed in to snuggle with Cecelia.

"What, no baby?" she asked.

"She's getting bigger, sleeping longer."

Cecelia muttered something, but I think she was already back to sleep. I snuggled in and held her close, a soft little spoon to my big spoon as I curled around her.

I woke up several hours later to Georgie's giggles. I rubbed the sleep from my eyes and sat up. My movement caused Georgie to fall onto her bottom and then fall sideways. She giggled even more.

"Dada's awake," Cecelia announced and clapped her hands.

Georgie struggled to right herself and then crawled over to me. She crawled up my arm, grabbing onto my shirt for support.

"That's okay, isn't it? To have her call you Dada?" Cecelia asked.

I nodded and pulled Georgie into my lap. I buzzed a kiss to the top of her head. "Yeah, I've gotten used to it. I've gotten used to her." I looked up and my gaze locked with Cecelia's. I reached out to touch her and caught the edge of her shirt sleeve. "And you, too."

She leaned over and pulled my hand to her face. "I missed you so much. And I am so happy to see you. But I don't know what to do." She sounded stressed.

I tugged on her sleeve and shifted against the headboard so I could wrap an arm around her and still hold onto Georgie.

Cecelia tucked in next to me and started playing with Georgie's feet.

I didn't think I would ever get enough of this, the three of us tucked up into bed together. This was so much more of a family moment than anything I could remember as a kid. I certainly had never been allowed in my parents' room, let alone crawl into bed with them at the same time. I never saw my mother in her night clothes and never saw my father in his pajamas until the last few months of his life when he was too sick to be able to complain about propriety.

"Talk to me, Cecelia. What's wrong?"

"The same thing as always. My stupid job. There is no way that Reina isn't going to tell everyone that some guy with a baby showed up looking for me or that I wasn't there all night. If they find out I'm seeing you again, that's the end of my job."

"Would Reina really tell on you?"

Cecelia shrugged. "Hard to tell. She's self-centered and super entitled. Maybe she didn't even notice. No, she would have noticed enough so that she could take over my room. I can just hear her now, 'But I thought you were gone,' when I go back and ask why she's in my room."

"Don't go back there," I said.

Cecelia sighed. "They'll fire me if I don't. I've been looking for another job in Dallas for weeks now, and I haven't gotten a single response to any of the applications I've submitted."

"Let them fire you."

"What?"

"Let them. No, better yet, quit. You don't need that job."

"Sterling, I may not need *that* job, but I need a job. I have bills and rent. This may come as a surprise to you, but unlike you, I'm not a trust fund baby."

I laughed at her sense of humor.

"What if we didn't have to sneak around?" I asked.

Cecelia leaned into my chest with a heavy sigh. "That would be amazing."

"I sense a but coming?" I prompted.

It was her turn to laugh. "It's a big but."

"I like your big butt," I growled and leaned in to place a kiss on the side of her neck.

She cringed with a giggle, folding in on herself so I couldn't quite reach her neck. "Sterling."

I landed the kiss and a second one.

She wiggled away from me and slid off the bed. "I've got to get ready for work."

I tucked Georgie in and rolled, making a grab for Cecelia. I missed her as she slipped away. Georgie giggled, so I rolled again, landing on my back. I lifted Georgie up above me. She thought this was great fun and continued to giggle and have a good time.

The shower started, and I lost my moment with Cecelia. I rolled and set Georgie into the crib while I pulled out an applesauce pack to feed to her. They were gone. I looked in the trash. Yep, It looked like Cecelia had fed the baby. Damn, I loved that woman.

I stared at the bathroom door and then back at the baby. If I stepped in while Cecelia was in the shower, I'd climb in with her and make love to her.

Georgie complained and rattled the sides of the crib.

"I know, baby, I know. Not while you're awake."

I got dressed and played with the baby while I waited for Cecelia to get out of the bathroom.

She stepped out from the bathroom, dressed in the skirt to the little gray suit I saw her in so many times. Her top was pink, and her hair was wrapped in a towel turban style, and she was the most beautiful I had ever seen because she was here with me.

"You should probably give me a ride back to the apartment so I can take my car in," she said.

"I can give you a ride."

She shook her head. "They'll see you, they'll—"

"Let them, Cecelia. Better yet, I'll walk in with you and you can tell them you quit."

She opened her mouth to protest. I stepped across the small space and pulled her to me. "Quit work. Take care of me and Georgie."

"I'm not a nanny, Sterling."

"I don't want a nanny, Cecelia. I want you in my life. When you said you were coming here to Amarillo, I thought we could make it work. Long weekends together, meeting in the middle where no one would know us. I see now that it won't work. It's not fair to you. If it means you don't work for them, then don't."

Her smile faltered.

"I know you want a job and to be able to take care of yourself. But let me take care of you. You can find another job."

"My apartment. I have to pay rent."

I shook my head. "If you won't move in with us, then I'll help you until you find another job."

"Wait, stop. What did you say?" she asked.

"Let me take care of you," I repeated.

"No, the move in with you part. You want me to move in with you?" She looked so scared.

I smiled and nodded. "Yes, Cecelia. I want you to live with me. Me and Georgie. And before you come up with any other excuses, I will put you on my insurance, I'll add you to my cellphone plan. I want you with me. We are a family. We belong together."

She gulped and a tear ran down her cheek.

"I need you," I confessed.

Georgie crawled across the bed and tried to get to her feet. She wobbled and fell into a sitting position. She held her arms up to Cecelia, asking to be picked up. "Mama."

"We need you."

Cecelia lifted Georgie and cradled her in close. I wrapped my arms around both of them. "Georgie needs a mother. She needs you."

38

CECELIA

Emotions overwhelmed me, and I cried. I was so happy and I was crying. I should have been laughing and dancing. Instead, I was a snotty mess. My skin had to have been splotchy, and I desperately needed a tissue.

I held onto Georgie and leaned into Sterling. These two were my everything. I was going to have a real family.

"Come on, let's get out of here. Let's go home," Sterling said.

I pulled the towel I had wrapped around my hair off and wiped my face. "I still need to quit my job."

"Call them from the road," Sterling said. It was a logical choice.

"I should give them back the keys."

"Keys?"

I nodded. "To that apartment. If you and Georgie want—"

"No, we're staying with you."

"But I need to drive my car back. There's no reason to wait for me," I said.

"Do you think I'm letting you out of my sight now that I have you back?" He stroked his knuckle down the side of my face. "We can go get breakfast. I'll drive you in to the office. I'll wait for you if you don't want me by your side when you hand the keys over, and I will reluctantly drive you back to your car so that I can follow you back to Dallas."

I sighed. Yeah, back to Dallas. "And what happens then?"

Sterling's brow crinkled up and he gave a quick shake. "We go home. My home, our home."

"Do you think I could swing by my apartment to pick up some other clothes? I'm getting so sick of the same outfits day after day." And these clothes were starting to get uncomfortable. Not tight or snug, but I had this building fullness in my lower stomach and it made certain clothes not feel very good.

I needed to tell Sterling.

"That all sounds good."

"Let's get out of here."

It didn't take very long to gather our items and check out of the hotel once I was finished getting ready. I didn't bother to dry my hair. I just braided it and let it air dry. And since I wasn't going to stay at work once I got to the office, I changed out of the skirt and top and put on leggings and a tunic. I was much more comfortable.

We stopped for breakfast at a diner. Georgie was a happy baby, and I was going to be her mother, or her guardian, or... My heart could hardly contain the emotions that stirred up in me. I may not have had the words to define what we were going to be, but family was the word that felt the most right.

My phone rang, and I looked at the caller ID. I shrugged and returned to eating my omelet. It rang again.

"Do you need to get that?" Sterling asked.

I shook my head. "It's work. They are probably wondering where I am. If I answer it, they'll pretend to be concerned, but when I get in, they'll threaten me with—" I started laughing. "They'll threaten to fire me. It's such a stupid threat. I mean, it's just a job, and not a very good one at that. No wonder someone sabotaged their servers before I started working there. They treat everyone like crap."

Sterling shrugged. "Yeah, I can see that."

He paid the bill and tipped handsomely to make up for the mess that Georgie made. More of her food seemed to be on the floor than I think made it into her mouth.

My nerves were on edge the entire drive to the office park where work was located. The flips in my stomach were either breakfast not sitting well, or anxiety, or… "Pull over!" I yelled.

"What?"

"Pull over, now." I convulsed with the need to throw up. Sterling stopped the car, and I vaulted out my door and doubled over. I lost my breakfast completely.

"Cecelia?" Sterling came around the side of the car and put his hand on my back. He handed me some napkins.

"Do you have any water in there?" I asked, waving at the car.

He nodded and pulled a water bottle from the back. "I started keeping a full diaper bag's worth of all the extras in the car."

I cracked the lid open and swished my mouth out with the first sip, spitting on the ground. I then took slow, careful swallows.

"This job has you all wired up. I never realized how upset it made you. I should have paid better attention, should have offered to help you out so you could quit earlier." He looked concerned as he ran his hand up and down my arm.

I loved that he wanted to help me out, loved it so much. "This isn't the job. And I should probably tell you before I get there and go marching in there and quit."

"Sounds serious. Let's get you back in the car." He helped me climb in, and he pulled the belt over me, leaning in to buckle me in.

I grazed my hand through his hair and held onto his arm, not letting him move away. I took a deep breath and let it out slowly. "I'm pregnant, Sterling. You're going to be a father."

He didn't move, didn't say anything. He stared at me for a moment. Just as I expected him to get angry with me, a slow smile spread across his lips. He started laughing. "Are you serious?"

I bit my lip and nodded.

"I thought you were on birth control?" A dozen emotions crossed his face in the flicker of seconds. His brows scrunched together, then they separated and lifted. His eyes narrowed before opening wide and then narrowing again. And he couldn't stop smiling.

"I was. Clearly, it's not perfect. I'm sorry I didn't tell you right away, but I..."

"You're pregnant? I'm going to be a father?" He stepped back from the car and ran his hand through his hair. "Georgie's gonna be a big sister?"

I nodded. I hadn't thought of it that way, but I was still getting used to the idea that I was going to help raise her. "Of course, we'll raise them as sisters."

Sterling rushed back to me and tried to wrap his arms around me. The stupid seat belt was in the way.

I managed to get unbuckled, and he pulled me out of the car and into his arms. His hands kept running over my hair and my face.

"You're going to have my baby?"

I nodded.

He dropped to his knees and put his hands on my hips, carefully pressing his face into my stomach. He looked up at me, and tears were in his eyes.

I reached out to brush his cheek, but he captured my hand and pressed his lips to my knuckles.

My heart was so full of love for him. This reaction was so much better than I could have imagined.

"This is amazing. We'll have to up the timeline on the wedding," he said.

"Wedding?" My mouth went dry. "Wedding? Sterling, what wedding?"

"Ours. You, me, we're getting married. What did you think I meant when I said Georgie needs a mother?"

"I... I..." I shrugged.

Sterling was on his feet, cupping my face. "I love you, Cecelia. I want you to be my wife, and we're going to have a family."

"I... I... Yes, Sterling, yes." I started to laugh, and then he was kissing me.

"I love you," I said. I finally was able to tell him, and I felt like I could fly. It was such an amazing feeling. "I love you." I didn't want to stop saying it.

"I love you," he said. The sound of his voice rumbling over those words made my toes curl.

We stood there laughing and holding each other for I don't know how long before Georgie started howling.

We broke apart, and Sterling stepped over and opened the back door. She didn't stop crying until he pulled her out of her car seat. He bounced as he walked and carried her over to me. "Mama's gonna have a baby. You're going to be a big sister."

He handed her to me, and she settled.

"She was mad that she was stuck in the car," he said.

"She's gonna be madder to be stuck in the car all day," I pointed out.

Sterling nodded. "She did pretty good on the drive up here. She'll fall asleep soon enough. Come on, let's get those keys back, and we can get on with the rest of our lives."

He smiled. It made my heart flip. I couldn't wait to start my life with him.

* * *

"Oh, Cecelia, where have you been? Marcy is all kinds of bitchy that you're late," Brittany, the receptionist, said as I walked in.

"Well, she can be as cranky and pissed off as she wants. I don't care." I put the keys to the apartment on the counter in front of her desk. "She's not a threat to me."

Brittany snorted. "She's going to get you fired for this."

I shook my head. "She can't fire me. I don't work here anymore. Can I borrow that pen?"

She slapped the pen on the tall counter that surrounded her desk. I grabbed one of the cheap pads of paper that were sitting there as a free gift to visitors. I scribbled down Sterling's address, my address. And then I wrote, *I Quit* across the bottom and handed her the entire pad.

"Have HR send my last paycheck to this address." I turned and walked out.

39

STERLING

My nerves were on edge, and I wasn't the one walking into that office to quit. I leaned against the SUV, door open so that I could hear Georgie and peek in if she complained and needed to see me. I knew how she felt. I wanted Cecelia to walk back out and be done with this already.

I was too old to be excited like a little kid, but I was. I was eager for us to finally be together the way we were meant to be. Husband, wife, child, a family.

She pushed out from the double glass doors that hid me from view, and she swayed her hips like she was feeling good, on top of the world. I swept her into my arms. Her smile was infectious, and it was hard to kiss while I was smiling like a fool.

"I've been thinking," I started.

"That's good, your brain works. I think mine's been in some numb holding pattern for so long, I don't know if I can think."

She was feeling good, sassing off and making jokes.

"Damn, I have missed you," I confessed.

"I missed you so much, but now, I don't have to worry about that stupid job."

"Good, that's one conflict of interest we no longer have to deal with," I said.

"What do you mean, that's one? There are more? I mean, my working there and seeing you, yeah, definitely, but…?"

"I did tell you my lawyer is suing to get their records and to release the information they have regarding Georgie's biological father." I looked over at her as I started the car up and began navigating out of the parking lot.

"You might have. We've said a lot of words in the past twelve hours, and I have to admit I'm pretty much stuck on two things." She let out a nervous giggle.

"Only two?"

"You love me," she said. Her smile lit up my entire world.

"I do. I do love you, Cecelia."

"And—hey, where are you going? We have to go back and get my car!" She braced her hands against the door and the dash as if I needed to slam on the brakes.

I let out a heavy breath. It slipped my mind. I had her with me, where she belonged. I was headed home. "Is there anything you really need in it right now?"

"Yeah, it's my car. I'm going to need it."

I shook my head. "No, you won't. You can use the car service. Or you can borrow my car."

"Sterling!"

"For a few days. Is there anything you need in your car that you will need this week? Do you have everything with you that you need to take back to Dallas right now?"

"Yeah, I guess," she answered, but she still sounded perplexed.

"I'll get someone to drive your car back," I said.

"Yes, me. I'll drive my car back. It's less of a bother, and you won't have to pay someone a ridiculous amount of money to get back up here just to drive my car."

"It is a bother. I want you with me and Georgie." I stopped her before she could properly protest. "And it's worth whatever it will cost to have you in that seat next to me for the next six to seven hours. Or however long this will take us."

"I can't afford—"

"I can. You are going to have to get used to a different way of thinking about money. It's a tool."

"It's a precious commodity when you don't have a lot of it. And I grew up being mindful of my spending."

"And I grew up using money as a tool to leverage situations to my benefit," I admitted.

"See, very different. So don't chastise me when I think of ways of saving money," she said fiercely.

"Fair enough. I'll keep that in mind if you keep in mind that money is a means of saving time. I want to spend as much time with you as I can, so if that means I pay someone to fly to Amarillo, spend the night at a nice hotel, and then spend the next day driving your car back to Dallas, to me, that's worth every penny."

"Really? You'd spend all of that just so we can stare at the same highway from the same car? You know we'd be looking at the same road if I were in my car following you back to Dallas, and it wouldn't even cost you the price of gas."

I reached across and picked up her hand. "But I wouldn't be able to touch you, wouldn't be able to glance over and see that little smile on your face that lets me know you're happy. Your smile is priceless to me."

She blushed and glanced down to where our fingers were intertwined.

"You're blushing. What did I say?" I asked. I hadn't said anything that could be taken as a double-entendre or blatant, sexualized flirting. She blushed at the most random of times.

I kept glancing over at her and then returning my attention to the road. I wanted to watch her, see how her eyes would lift up to me, how her lids would flicker and her lashes flutter. But I had to keep an eye on the road at the same time. She was distracting. But she would be equally as distracting if she were in her own car, because I would constantly want to make sure she was all right. And frankly, the phone service through rural Texas was not good enough for us to keep the phone lines open so we could talk the entire time.

"That was really romantic, that's all," she said in a small, almost shy voice.

"You like romantic words, do you?" I grinned.

She surprised me yet again. Smooth talking and sweet words could make her blush. She liked to talk dirty in bed. She wasn't willing to let me get away with anything simply because I said so or I could pay my way through a situation. She kept me on my toes, offered tiny challenges so I had to pay attention. She was smart, funny, and so beautiful and soft. I couldn't have found a more perfect woman if I had been looking for one.

She bit her lip and nodded. "Okay, you win, especially when you put it like that and sweet talk me. But I'm still right," she teased.

"Darling, you will always be right, but you had better get used to the fact that I always get my way." I took my hand back and continued to drive.

Her jaw dropped and she made an offended sound.

"You're in the car with me. And we are leaving your car behind, and you think it's romantic and sweet." I chuckled.

She started laughing. "Yes, it is sweet. I can't think of a time anyone would ever have been willing to give up that kind of money just to be in my company."

"You clearly never worked as an escort," I teased.

Cecelia dropped my hand and swatted at my arm. "You are incorrigible!"

"I speak the truth. You would have made a killing as an escort."

"Shut up, Sterling. I would not. Look at me."

"I'd love to, but I'm driving."

"I'm not what men would look for in a date for hire." She shook her head and crossed her arms.

From what I could see in my peripheral vision, she looked like she was pouting. "I didn't say prostitute, I said escort. Big difference. You are witty, and men want someone they can take out in public who can hold up a conversation."

"They want someone they can show off, a model. They don't want someone built like me," she complained.

"I want someone built like you. I want you. Men want someone who looks good and can turn heads. You do that. You have beautiful hair, and your smile lights up the world. And you dress up beautifully. I'm not talking about the kinds of clothes you wear to work, but that dress you wore the last time I took you out." I reached over and skimmed a knuckle over the top swells of her breasts, grazing her softness through her shirt. "These were exceptional. Trust me, you have all the right elements. And I know when I take you out and show you off, other men will be envious of what I have."

"You really think that?"

I nodded. "Definitely. I am a very lucky man."

"I'm the lucky one," she said.

She relaxed and shifted in her seat. She turned ever so slightly so she could look at me. "Do you really want to marry me?" she asked.

"Definitely."

"And you didn't just ask because I'm pregnant?"

I gripped the steering wheel a bit harder before pulling the car off to the side of the road. The car bumped over the detritus on the side of the road, and the front tire left the pavement before we came to a complete stop. I put the car in park and turned to look at her. I picked up her hands and held them to my chest, to my heart.

"I apparently hadn't made myself clear earlier when I said that Georgie needed a mother. That was me saying I wanted to marry you. I should have proposed more properly, with a ring, and not on the side of the road."

"I think your proposal was wonderful. I just didn't want you to think—"

I put a finger to her lips to stop the worrisome thought. "Shh, I love you. That's all that matters." I replaced my finger with my lips. "Let's go home."

40

CECELIA

Six hours stuck in a car with Sterling didn't feel like much time at all. We flirted and talked about nothing. It was wonderful.

"I want you to move in right away," Sterling said.

"Okay. My apartment is pretty small, but I still have furniture and stuff to move."

"Do you really need your furniture?"

"What's that supposed to mean? Yes, I need a place to sit down and a table to eat at and do my craft projects," I pointed out.

"I have couches and tables, and my bed is infinitely bigger and more comfortable than yours," he pointed out. "Keeping that in mind, what do you need to keep? Anything sentimental or given to you by your parents?"

"I don't have parents," I blurted out.

"Everyone has parents." Sterling chuckled.

"Georgie doesn't," I pointed out.

"She does. She has us. We're her parents. We will be her parents."

I blinked back tears. I loved that so much. I let out a long, slow breath through pursed lips. "Well, she's lucky. I wasn't. I was Georgie. My bio-mom had me young, no clue who my bio-father was. At some point, she took off and left me with a cousin."

"A cousin?" Sterling asked.

"Technically, my grandmother's cousin, so kind of like an aunt, I guess. Anyway, my extended family had me, and they resented being saddled with me. They made sure I knew I was a burden every day of my life. I walked out the door and never looked back the day after high school graduation. It's why I pushed you so hard at first. It's why I even suggested that it would be better to give her up if you couldn't be bothered to really take care of her."

I wiped my face and looked out the side window at the low scrub and dirt rolling past.

Sterling put his hand on my leg. "I didn't know."

"How could you? It's not exactly something I go around telling people. It's why I went into social services. I want to help people. I know the foster care system is seriously broken. It needs a complete overhaul, but it does do some good. There are kids out there who end up with forever families who want them. And there are people like you. You really just didn't know what you were doing, but your heart was in the right place."

"I really was, no, I really am still clueless about what I am doing when it comes to Georgie, but I love her, and I want to be the best father I can for her."

"That counts for a lot, Sterling. That counts for a whole lot."

Two weeks later...

242

The elevator doors slid open. I carried the last box of stuff from my apartment into the penthouse. I didn't know exactly where I would put it. It wasn't that I had a lot of stuff—I didn't—or that the penthouse was small—it wasn't. But combining two households filled up space.

Almost all of my furniture was donated to a women's shelter.

Sterling didn't do garage sales, and my stuff was barely good enough for that, but it was better than junk to set out on the curb, so we donated it. He wanted to keep the dinette set I had. It was old and Formica with vinyl covered chairs. Mid-Century standard kitchen design. Apparently, Sterling had a preference for Mid-Century furniture. I should have guessed looking at the interior décor of his place. Then again, I hadn't really gotten much past *big* and *no baby furniture*.

I'd learned a lot in the last two weeks of living with him. He did have a style preference, and he liked good food. And even though all the overflow of my belongings were taking over his home gym as a storage space, he seemed to really like my being here.

I loved it. I had a family, one that wanted me. One that I loved with my whole heart.

"What are you doing?" Sterling asked. He took a few steps toward me and took the box out of my hands. "You're pregnant. Why are you carrying boxes?"

"It's not that heavy, and it's not boxes, it's box, singular. The last one. I'm officially all moved in. Well, until tomorrow when I drop the keys off at the leasing office."

"You should have told me you needed to move more stuff. I would have gotten you a work crew or an assistant."

"Last box. It's just last-minute junk. I didn't need a moving crew."

He glowered and grumbled at me. "You're my wife and—"

"Not for another week, I'm not. Sterling, you have the box under one arm. It's not heavy," I pointed out.

He hefted it, testing the lack of weight. "Where do you want it?"

"I was going to take it downstairs to add it to my pile in the gym. Sorry about that." I did feel bad for taking over his space. He was making room for me in his home. I had to remember that I wasn't impinging upon him. He asked for it, literally.

I followed as he began walking in that direction.

"It's quiet around here. Georgie asleep?" I had been out running errands and getting the last few things from my apartment all morning.

"Nanny Fletcher has taken her to the park. I need to go into the office, put out a few fires."

"You still have time left on your leave, don't you?" He should have been able to take twelve weeks off based on the Family Medical Leave Act, but I didn't know what his company's policy was beyond that.

"I'm due back on a regular basis in another week, but I'm taking a much-needed vacation immediately."

"Vacation?"

He placed the box on top of one of the many stacks that I was going to have to start digging through and finding homes for everything.

"Yes, vacation." He turned, and his arms slid around my hips, pulling me in close. I loved being in his arms. "More like a honeymoon."

"Honeymoon? You're taking me on a honeymoon?" My eyes went wide, and I dropped my jaw. We hadn't discussed going on a honeymoon. We had talked about wedding plans, and neither of us could see any reason we should wait any longer than it took his lawyers to draw up a prenuptial agreement. I had insisted, much to Sterling's lawyer's relief.

The wedding was going to be small—an officiant, Wayne, Georgie, and Nanny Fletcher. The zoo administration said we could have the ceremony by the tiger exhibit as long as we kept it small. So, first thing in the morning in the middle of the week when the zoo was full of mommies and babies, we were going to get married.

"What about Georgie? She's too young to leave with someone she doesn't know."

Sterling smiled wide. "She's coming with. I couldn't see any way we could leave her. You're right, she's too young. And I can't legally take her out of the state. Not until her custody situation is cleared up and finalized. I've gotten us a cabin by a lake. It's only for a few days, but I thought it would be good enough. When the kids are older and we have someone we can trust to watch them overnight, I'll take you to Rome or Paris. Wherever you want."

"Really, wherever? So if I said I wanted to go to Oklahoma?"

His brow crinkled up. "You want to go to Oklahoma for your honeymoon?"

I shook my head and laughed. "Not really, but if that's what I wanted?"

"Then, yes, I'll take you to Oklahoma if that's what you want."

"It's not. Just testing the waters, so to speak. Dubai? Tokyo? Mauritius?"

"Mauritius?" Sterling laughed.

"Dodo birds," I explained. "I know they don't exist, but I've always wanted to see the home of Dodo birds."

"We'll take a trip every year, and you can choose the place," he said. "We can go everywhere."

"Or nowhere?" I cupped the side of his face. "Cabin by a lake?"

He nodded. "Let's start with nowhere and go from there."

I tipped my face up, inviting him in for a kiss. He obliged me immediately. His lips were soft and warm. He held me tighter, and his firm muscles pressed against me.

"We could always just stay here," he growled into my mouth.

"That's a fun idea. How soon before Nanny Fletcher gets back with Georgie?"

"Too soon to do anything properly this afternoon," he complained.

"We can always put Georgie to bed early," I suggested.

Sterling pressed his face into the sensitive spot along my neck. I flinched and giggled as he kissed and tickled me. "That sounds like a brilliant idea. Let's put Georgie to bed early, and we can start the honeymoon tonight."

"I think we started the honeymoon two weeks ago," I said around my laughter.

"So much lost time to make up for." He planted a firm kiss on my lips and eased his grip on me. "I love you, Cecelia Alexander. That name sounds good. One more week."

"And I love you. I think husband sounds pretty good too."

41

EPILOGUE

STERLING

A year later…

"Mommy." Georgie ran up to Cecelia. I strode in behind her.

Cecelia looked up from gazing down at the baby, something she seemed to do a lot more than I ever could have expected. The baby was still so tiny at barely three months old. To be honest, when I held her, I also spent a good amount of time just watching her little face.

Georgie had been small when she came into my life, but she hadn't been as tiny as Ashley. There was something truly intimidating about an infant.

"Shh, Ashley just fell asleep," Cecclia said quietly.

Georgie climbed up on the couch next to Cecelia and wedged herself so that she was able to stare at her baby sister and still be on her mother's lap without pushing the baby out of the way. They were still working on sharing Mommy's personal space.

Cecelia didn't have much since the baby was born. Ashley was still very much an extension of her mother, relying on her for everything, her source of nutrition and comfort. And at times, Georgie was very jealous of Ashley.

Cecelia never lost her cool. Not once. She also didn't lie to Georgie. Whenever Georgie asked if she came out of Mommy's tummy, we had agreed to always be honest with her, but not in a harmful way. So we told Georgie she was in a different mommy's tummy, but she was Cecelia's baby too.

In time, she would ask about that other mommy, and that's when she would learn about her mother. I loved my sister and missed her. And I realized I missed the idealization of Argene since I really didn't know her well. I would make sure that Georgie knew just how special her mother had been.

"How was class?" Cecelia asked.

"We danced and played with little shaker instruments," I said as I lifted Georgie a bit so I could sit next to all of my girls at once.

Georgie and I had spent our morning at a daddy-and-me music class for toddlers. It was interesting how many men there were literally pushed by their baby mamas into the classroom with the kid in tow. Some were there happily and willingly so their wives and partners could have some quiet at home with the new baby. It was an interesting dynamic and a completely different world than I knew existed two years ago.

I kissed Georgie on the head. She had brought all of this wonderful change into my life.

"How was your morning?" I asked.

"It's been quiet. Like this. Ashley was a bit fussy earlier, so I've been holding her."

"You want me to take her so you can go rest?"

Cecelia shook her head, her gaze still on the sleeping baby. "I'm good."

"You're better than good." I leaned across Georgie, who squirmed and complained, to kiss Cecelia on the temple.

I stood and picked Georgie up with me. She started to fight and fuss. "Mommy has to take care of the baby, so we have to take care of Mommy. Let's go make her lunch."

Georgie curled up her lips in a pout. I wanted to laugh at how serious she looked.

"If Mommy gets lunch and has a rest, she can play with Georgie later, okay?"

She nodded, her little lips still pursed.

Wayne was in the kitchen chopping something when we walked in.

"What do we have that's good for lunch?" I asked.

"With Miss Cecelia's dietary restrictions, may I suggest a light chicken salad?" he said.

"Sounds good, do we have that?" I set Georgie down in her chair. She still had the same high chair, only now, we no longer bothered buckling her in. She knew how to sit up. It was easier with the tray right at her level.

"You want some crackers?" I asked Georgie.

She nodded and said "Fid acker." Fish cracker. All those noises she made as a baby were finally now turning into words. And surprisingly enough, I could understand it all.

I placed a handful of goldfish crackers on the tray and grabbed a juice box just as she started demanding "duce".

She took the box and sucked on the straw before cramming another couple of crackers into her mouth. It was a good thing she was so cute. She was a sloppy eater.

"Would you mind watching Georgie for a few minutes?" I asked Wayne.

"Of course not," he said, looking over his shoulder at her from his prep work.

"Don't let her handle any of the knives," I said as I gave her another kiss. At some point in time, hopefully not for many, many years, she would shrug away from my kisses and say something like, 'Ew, Dad, gross.' Until then, I planned on kissing the top of her head as often as I could.

Cecelia still sat in the living room staring at the sleeping Ashley.

"Sweetheart, let's put her down. You are exhausted." I reached down and lifted Ashley from my wife's arms. Cradling the baby in one arm, I eased Cecelia to her feet and took her hand.

The house, which we moved into about three months before Ashley was born, was large, and the rooms were spread farther apart than they had been in the penthouse. But the terrace, as lovely as it was, was not a safe place for small children to play. They didn't need to grow up in a glass tower when I could easily buy them a castle with a playground. The house wasn't exactly a castle, but I had filled it with my princesses.

I carried Ashley upstairs and into our bedroom. Ashley still mostly co-slept with us, but there was a crib set off to the side of the room for when she napped. I gently placed her in the crib and adjusted the blanket so it would help to keep her propped sleeping on her side.

Cecelia was already sitting on the edge of our bed when I could finally give her my full attention. I slid to my knees in front of her and wrapped my arms around her waist, resting my head on her lap.

She gently stroked my hair.

"Did you really have a good time in class?" she asked quietly.

"I did. It was fine," I answered. It was fine. And when Ashley was older, I'd take her to those classes too.

"You are the most amazing father, you know that?"

I chuckled. "You wouldn't have said that a year ago."

Cecelia hissed. "A year ago was rough. But look at how far we've come. We have two amazing baby girls. Wayne didn't quit when I moved in, or when we got this place."

"It's been a good year. But I know it hasn't always been easy."

Cecelia leaned over, hugging my head. "I know. It's been a struggle. But it's almost over, right? Another… what, month or two?"

I shifted, and she sat up so I could lift my head. I beamed up at her. My smile felt like it was going to break my face. I had been holding on to this information so I could share it just between the two of us.

"What?" She began to smile in reaction to my smile.

I reached into my back pocket and pulled out a folded pack of papers. "I've literally been sitting on this for days. I was trying to save it for our anniversary. But I can't wait any longer."

"That's in two days. You couldn't wait two more days?" she teased.

"I guess I can." I started to put the paperwork back into my pocket.

Cecelia grabbed my arm. "Oh, no, you don't. You don't get to tease me like that. What is it?"

I sat back on my heels and spread the papers out, unfolding them. These were just photocopies. I had the originals secure in a document safe.

"She's ours. It's official. The judge wanted to make us wait the full four months for parental abandonment after the suit was settled. But Chavez's team worked their magic, and they showed the judge that we did due diligence. They presented proof that there were two independent teams trying to locate Georgie's bio-father during the time of the lawsuit. And we had the settlement from the suit with the fraud charges against the agency. The judge agreed we could back date the abandonment. She's ours. We have full custody, and he went ahead and confirmed the adoption.

Cecelia shifted through the pages. Unless she read them, they didn't make a whole lot of sense, lots of legalese language about a civil suit on how Georgie's case was mishandled. I flipped through the corners until I found the one I wanted Cecelia to look at. I pulled it out and placed it on top of the small stack.

Cecelia ran her fingers over the lines of text as she read. Tears pooled in her eyes, and she covered her mouth as she began to cry. I climbed up on the bed next to her and wrapped my arms around her.

The words that made her cry were our names in the spaces naming the parents on Georgie's amended birth certificate.

"She's really ours? No one can take her?" I felt Cecelia's words in my heart. It had been an unspoken fear we had to endure for months longer than we should ever have had to.

The agency that was overseeing Georgie's custody for Argene's estate had mismanaged us completely. I would forever be thankful they brought Georgie and Cecelia into my life, but they were committing fraud. Nothing like adoption fraud, but they had dragged out the investigation and time spent under their watchful management to scam more money out of the estate. They kept saying they had found the bio-father when they really hadn't. That civil suit had impacted the custody situation, turning it into a battle instead of the easy transfer it should have been.

"I love you. Happy anniversary." I kissed my wife on the temple.

She raised a tear-streaked face to me, and I kissed her on the lips.

"This is the most amazing present ever. I love you, Sterling. Maybe we should put the girls to bed early tonight?"

I kissed my wife again. "I love the way you think."

42

EXCERPT: HIS TO OWN

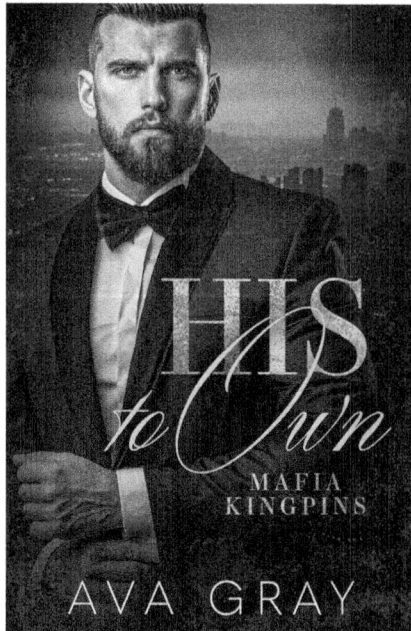

He's supposed to marry her older sister, but he can't stay away...

MICELI

The mafia world is cold and cruel. I live by one rule - cut their throat before they cut yours. It's what keeps me ruthless and on top of my mafia family.

But when I see something I like, I take it. It's no different with Alessia DeLuca, who's supposed to marry my rival... while I'm marrying her older sister.

When Alessia sees something she shouldn't, kidnapping her is the only logical answer...

Taking her cherry sure isn't.

ALESSIA

Ever since I met him in a mix-up, I've been intrigued by Miceli Rossi. He says he always gets what he wants, and it's obvious he's obsessed with one thing only... me.

He can force me to marry him. He can even force me to wear his ring.

But I'll make sure I'm the worst wife he could have.

Anything to make sure he doesn't realize how much I want him.

His to Own is book one of the Mafia Kingpins series. This is a full-length standalone novel with these tropes: age gap, mafia, V-card, surprise pregnancy. Guaranteed happy ending!

Alessia

I've never been so nervous in all of my twenty-four years. Pacing across the room again, I know I must be wearing a trail in the carpet, and I finally pause and wring my hands. My older sister Gia—older by two years—doesn't look even a fraction as anxious as me.

A quick glance at the clock reveals it's only a couple of minutes until eleven.

"How can you be so calm?" I ask. "I'm about to pass out or poo my pants. And you look like you're about to take tea on the lido deck."

She snorts back a laugh. "Because, sis, there's no point in getting worked up. Our fate has already been decided." Gia flips her long, dark hair over a shoulder and sends me a perfect smile. And it is flawless. Everything about Gia is—from her slender figure to her high cheekbones to her polished and refined manners. She should've been a model. Or, the queen of some faraway country. I swear, sometimes I wonder if she sweats or burps or ever feels like she's going to poo her pants like me? She's a classic beauty and always appears so in control. Even when she's not.

Me, on the other hand? I'm a hot mess. I worry, I stress and I obsess. That, of course, leads to the sugar cravings that I can't seem to control. Grabbing another piece of candy from the small bowl on my nightstand, I unwrap the watermelon deliciousness and pop it into my mouth, sucking until my cheeks cave.

"But, we're about to meet the men we're going to marry," I say with a frown. "Men we've never met."

Gia sighs in that worldly way of hers. "What do you need to know? They're both extremely handsome and powerful. An alliance between our family and both of theirs will secure the DeLuca name and increase our importance in this city."

Something I care very little about, but I don't say that. My father, Aldo DeLuca, is an important figure in New York City's Italian mafia. Although, he's not quite as powerful as The Rossi or Bianche family. That's why he's planning on marrying me off to Rocco Bianche and Gia to Miceli Rossi.

My stomach turns when I think about the stranger I'm about to go downstairs and meet. A man I'm just supposed to say "hello" to and then "I do" without any time to get to know him.

He's a stranger! I want to scream. This is so old-fashioned and ridiculous. Or, am I the one who's overreacting? Gia is quite content to marry Miceli and she's never laid eyes on the man. But, she's already had a serious boyfriend and been intimate with someone before. Maybe that's why this isn't as big of a deal for her. But, I've never been in love much less had a relationship and sex or explored any of that. God, I feel like such a baby. A naive little girl. Because the truth is it's more than just sex I've been missing out on. The truth is, I've never even been properly kissed by a man. I mean sure, there were a few quick kisses here or there when I was in school over in Italy. But those were boys who I met in town and saw a movie with. Now, I'm dealing with an experienced man who's going to have expectations and desires. How in the world am I ever going to please him?

Biting my lip, my frown deepens.

"Stop scowling like that," Gia comments. "Or you're going to make your wrinkles look deeper."

My head snaps up. "I have wrinkles?" I march over to the mirror and examine my face with a critical eye. Well, of course, I have frown lines between my brows. Doesn't everyone?

"Yes, Lessi, and the way you're always worrying, you're going to look like an old lady in a few years if you keep it up." She stands and stretches. "That's why I don't let anything bother me and use so many face creams."

Smoothing my index finger over the lines, I try to flatten them. I certainly don't want to look older than my years. Maybe I'm going to need to snag one of my sister's many potions or lotions. She's in the know about all the latest when it comes to looking younger and having gorgeous skin.

"Well, I suppose it's time to meet my fiancé," she says without a trace of emotion.

My heart rate kicks up and I start wringing my hands again.

Gia walks over and squeezes my arm. "You look like you're about to puke, Lessi. Relax. Why are you so worried, anyway? Just go downstairs and talk to the good-looking man for a little bit. Be agreeable, smile and laugh at his jokes. Easy, right?"

Easy for her maybe, but not for me. "Yeah, okay," I mumble. Watching Gia whirl away without a care in the world makes me green with envy. I wish I could be more like my sister. But we're pretty much opposites in every way. While she's tall and slender, I'm short and curvy. She's calm and easygoing, I'm anxious and high strung. And, she's a social butterfly. The boys at school all loved and chased her everywhere while I preferred to stay in my dorm and spend a quiet evening reading or studying.

Maybe I'm just wound too tight and being with Rocco Bianche will help loosen me up and learn to enjoy life more. But, for whatever reason, something about him doesn't feel right. Clasping a hand over my stomach, I wonder if I'm going to be sick. *Stop being so dramatic,* I scold myself. *Get it together and go down and meet your fiancé.*

Grabbing another piece of candy, I unwrap it and pop it into my mouth. I don't know why sucking on sweets calms me down—at least a little—but I pause and grab a handful of the candy, tucking them into my pocket. Better to be safe than sorry. Because I have a feeling I'm going to need every single one of them when I go face my husband-to-be...a complete and total stranger, as of this very moment.

Walking out of the safety and comfort of my bedroom, I head to the back staircase which will take me down to the library where Rocco is waiting. As I walk down the steps, I wonder if I should've dressed up more or put more makeup on? Gia looks like she just stepped off a runway and I look...well, like I always do. I didn't put any extra effort into my appearance and I wonder if that's because a part of me doesn't want Rocco to find me attractive? Because I want him to tell my father he isn't interested in marrying me.

Hmm. A devious, little plan begins to form in my brain. Maybe I should purposely try to turn him off. Do something unlady-like or be quiet and mousy, refusing to make polite conversation. Or...maybe I could tell him I'm in love with someone else. Make up a boyfriend and pretend I can't get married because I love someone else.

No, that won't work. He would probably just get annoyed and then go ask my father who would quickly deny the existence of my fictional man.

Standing right outside the library now, I hesitate, needing a moment to get myself together. Pushing my nerves down, I force myself to unclasp my hands and let them hang at my sides. Then, I pull in a deep, steadying breath and walk through the doorway.

A very tall man stands in front of the windows, his back to me. A very broad back with wide, muscular shoulders visible through his suit jacket that tense the moment he hears my soft footsteps on the carpet. The first thing I notice is the sharp cut of his lightly-stubbled jawline as turns and when he's fully facing me, my heart thumps harder. Holy hell, the man is insanely good-looking. I didn't expect to be face to face with a Greek adonis and I suck in a sharp breath.

With a naturally tanned complexion and thick, dark brown, slightly wavy hair slicked back off his gorgeous face, he makes me grab onto a nearby chair for support. Eyes darker than the deepest espresso focus on me and, maybe I'm imagining it, but I think I see approval. And maybe a wave of relief, too.

The other thing I immediately notice about him is he exudes power. And it has nothing to do with his perfectly-tailored black suit. It's the way he carries himself and the purposeful way he walks toward me. His vibe screams "I'm in charge" and you better listen to every word that comes out of my mouth.

Which, by the way, is a beautiful mouth. His lips look soft, very kissable, and the dark stubble gives him a dangerous look. It also makes me want to reach out and lay a hand against his cheek so I can feel its rough texture. The boys I've known were exactly that—boys with clean-shaven faces. This is a man in every sense of the word and when he extends a large hand, I glance down at it, suddenly at a loss and forgetting basic manners. I'm too fascinated by the groove that appears on his left cheek when he gives me a small smile. A freaking dimple that makes my stomach flip because it's the only thing about him that looks slightly boyish.

"It's nice to meet you," he says, voice so deep I can feel it rumble through my chest and roll all the way down, down, down to my toes.

"You, too," I force out as his huge hand encompasses mine like a softball mitt. Our gazes lock and I stare into eyes that are so dark brown they're almost black. Our hands hold for a moment too long and his intense gaze makes me uneasy. Uneasy and utterly mesmerized.

When he finally releases my hand, I let out a shaky breath.

"Shall we sit?"

I nod and follow him over to the couch. Keeping my distance, I carefully sit down a couple of feet away and instantly clasp my hands in my lap.

"You're not what I expected," he murmurs, his voice low and almost to himself.

I can feel him studying me and I shift under his thoroughly penetrating gaze. "Oh? And what did you expect?" I ask, daring to look over and up.

He leans closer, eyes narrowing slightly. "Not you."

When he doesn't elaborate, I can't help but burst out laughing. Maybe it's my nerves making me be inappropriate or maybe I'm starting to feel a tiny bit more comfortable in his powerful presence. Which is the oddest thing. How can I be feeling less anxiety when I should be feeling more? But something about him is almost...I don't know. Familiar? It makes no sense.

"What's so funny?" he asks, his eyes searching mine.

"I have to admit, I didn't expect this at all, either."

His mouth edges up and my attention zeroes in on that dimple. "Really?"

I nod, unable to stop smiling. Maybe this situation isn't as bad as I originally thought it would be. Marrying a stranger still scares the bejesus out of me, but if he's a calm, kind, gorgeous man who can put me at ease and take his time, be patient with me, then perhaps I'd be willing to try.

"I know this whole situation is awkward," he says, as though reading my mind. "And our families are being...pushy. But I want you to know, I'd never force a woman into marriage. If you're truly not interested in getting to know me better, I'll walk away."

"You would?" Of course, I lean forward and this makes me like him a little bit more.

"Before you make a final decision, you should know a few things first," he says, eyes bright and a little mischievous. "Some women consider me quite the catch."

"Oh, I'm sure," I say teasingly and chuckle. *Oh, my God, I'm flirting with him. And he's sitting here trying to sell himself.* A man like him doesn't need to convince a woman to be with him, but here he is being all adorable and a little unsure. And, I like that. Confidence is nice, but arrogance is a huge turn off to me. I'm glad that he's wondering and maybe not quite as self-assured as normal.

"That's right. They like the fact that I'm wealthy, powerful and, modesty aside, fairly attractive. That is, if you like the cliche." The way he says it makes me grin. Almost like he's making fun of himself.

"Cliche?"

"Tall, dark and handsome." He sends me a devastating smile.

Oh, I do! I scream internally. More so than I ever even realized. But, I play it cool and send him a smirk. "Oh, I don't know. Normally, I prefer short, fair and homely." He knows I'm joking and his eyes crinkle in the corners in the most adorable way.

"Really?" He huffs out a laugh.

I shrug a shoulder. "But, perhaps, I could be persuaded to expand my horizons."

He slides closer and my heart threatens to burst from my chest when his powerful thigh brushes mine. I'm holding my breath as he reaches for my hand, lifts it to his lips and brushes a kiss along my knuckles. "Then I'll do my best," he says in a low voice.

Swallowing hard, I bite down on my lower lip and a zap of awareness shoots through my body. The brief touch of his lips has me squeezing my thighs together and I can't seem to look away from his eyes. They're like a deep, dark swirling black hole, sucking me in deeper with every passing second.

The attraction between us is palpable and I smile. He's still holding my hand when he says, "So, Gia, tell me about yourself."

Gia? What is he talking about? *Oh, God.* My heart sinks as it belatedly occurs to my befuddled brain that I'm sitting here swooning over Miceli Rossi.

My sister's fiancé.

Oh, for God's sake. Then where the hell is the man I'm supposed to be marrying? And how am I ever expected to want him after meeting this amazing man?

"Um, I think there's been a mixup," I murmur, and his dark eyes narrow.

Read the full story HERE!

SUBSCRIBE TO MY MAILING LIST

I hope you enjoyed reading this book.

In case you would like to receive information on my latest releases, price promotions, and any special giveaways, then I would recommend you to subscribe to my mailing list.

You can do so now by using the subscription link below.

SUBSCRIBE TO AVA GRAY's MAILING LIST!

Printed in Dunstable, United Kingdom